Marisol and Magdalena

The Sound of Our Sisterhood

Veronica Chambers

HYPERION
PAPERBACKS FOR CHILDREN
NEW YORK

Por las mejores amigas
Jennie Gomez y mi mami

Y por mi abuela, Flora
who promised me a pollera

ACKNOWLEDGMENTS
My profound thanks to Steven Malk, Rita Holm, and the inimitable Sandra Dijkstra. Shay Youngblood inspires and encourages me. Andrea Davis Pinkney, *eres un milagro*. Junot Diaz speaks my language. I am grateful *por amigos buenos como* Miss Cassandra Butcher, Caroline Kim, Andrea Polans, Michael Trotman, Jennifer Yancey de la Fuente, Cathi Hanauer, and N'Gai Croal. *Gracias.*

And, as always, *un abundancia de cariños* to Lady Bug.
Shake what your mama gave you, girl.

The lyrics on pages 144–145 are from the song *Farolito*, written by Kike Santander. Lyrics copyright © 1995 Foreign Imported Productions & Publishing, Inc. (BMI). Reprinted by permission.

First Hyperion Paperback edition, 2001

A hardcover edition of *Marisol and Magdalena: The Sound of Our Sisterhood* is available from Jump at the Sun / Hyperion Books for Children.

Printed in the United States of America

1 3 5 7 9 10 8 6 4 2

The text for this book is set in 14-point Perpetua.

Library of Congress Cataloging-in-Publication Data

Chambers, Veronica.
Marisol and Magdalena: the sound of our sisterhood / Veronica Chambers.
    p.   cm.
Summary: Separated from her best friend in Brooklyn, thirteen-year-old Marisol spends a year with her grandmother in Panama where she secretly searches for her real father.
ISBN 0-7868-1304-0 (pbk.)
1. Panamanian Americans—Juvenile fiction. [1. Panamanian Americans—Fiction. 2. Best Friends—Fiction. 3. Grandmothers—Fiction. 4. Fathers and daughters—Fiction. 5. Panama—Fiction.] I. Title.
PZ7.C3575Mar   1998
[Fic]-dc21   97-34365
Visit hyperionchildrensbooks.com

1

Do you know what it's like to be in a room full of people, but to feel completely alone? Outside of the noise and the talking and the eating—just apart from it, watching it all? That's how I felt that night in the Rosarios' kitchen.

I've known the Rosario family since I was a little baby. I've been over to their house a million times. But that night it was like noticing it all for the first time. Noticing not just what everything looked like, but how it all felt. When I stopped to think about it, I realized how happy it all made me—these same things, these same people, that I have seen over and over again, my whole life long.

The Rosarios' kitchen is bright yellow. The wall by the stove is stained brown with oil that splatters from the stove. It's one of those kitchens that's like a magnet; whenever friends come over, everyone ends up in the kitchen. There is a long wooden counter where Magda was sitting on a tall stool, next to the *carimañolas*. My mother was rolling the meat into the batter and handing it over to Tía Luisa. The two of them were yakking away in Spanish; their hands flying as fast as their words.

Mami and Tía Luisa grew up together in Panama. Now we all lived in Brooklyn where Magda and I were born. We hung out at the Rosarios' every Friday night. Tía Luisa, Magdalena's mother, was a fabulous cook. She made delicious *frituras*—fried treats—which are more amazing than anything you could get at McDonald's or Burger King.

Tía Luisa made all kinds of unforgettable *frituras*: *carimañolas*, *tamales*, and *empanadas*, which are all different sorts of little pies with meat inside. *Carimañolas* are made of yucca; *empanadas* and *tamales* are made of corn. Tía Luisa filled them with chicken or beef; she even made vegetarian *tamales* when she got a special order.

All night long Panamanians from the neighborhood called on the phone and placed their orders. When Magda and I munched on too many *empanadas*, Tía Luisa would move the bowl of finished *frituras* to the other side of the stove. "You're eating all of my profits!" she would say. Mami said that Tía Luisa made good money cooking *frituras* because homesick Panamanians could never get enough of them.

Magda and I took turns answering the phone when it rang.

"Rosarios'!" we always said, singing the word as if we were working in a real restaurant.

Whenever I answered the phone, I could always tell that it was a Panamanian on the other line, because every Panamanian I ever met says "w'appin'?" instead of "hello." "W'appin'?" is short for "What's happening?"

I liked taking orders. I liked hearing the men and women say "*Dame* twelve *carimañolas*—that's twelve for Luisa." Or, "Save six *empanadas* with beef *con el nombre Edgar.*"

Their voices sound so much like Mami's and all my tías, so much like everyone I love, mixing English and Spanish—back and forth seamlessly, their language like a reversible sweater that you can wear on both sides.

When Magda and I weren't helping with the phones, or grating the yucca and the corn, we played waitress for the Rosarios' guests. Tío Ricardo, Magda's father, would invite a bunch of guys over to play dominoes in the basement of their house.

I love Tía Luisa, Magda's mother, but I love Tío Ricardo even more. I've never met my real father, and Tío Ricardo is like the *papi* I never had.

Mami doesn't like to discuss my real father. When she does, she uses words that are just a hair away from curse words. "*Sucio*," she calls him when she doesn't think I'm listening. But I know *sucio* means "dirty."

"*Sinvergüenza*" is another one and that means "good-for-nothing."

My father's name is Lucho Mayaguez. His real name is Luis, but whenever anybody talks about him, they call him Lucho. He lives in Panama. Mami says she hasn't heard from him since I was a baby. Mami says that he was a playboy, that she never thought their marriage would last. After she and my father got married, Mami came to the United States to live with Tía Julia. My father came, too, but he only stayed a year. "He said he didn't like New York," Mami once told me. "What he meant was he didn't like being married."

I think about my father a lot. I wonder what my life would be like if I knew him. I don't talk about it with Mami because she gets mad any time anyone brings up Lucho's name. I talk about my father with Magda, though. Sometimes she listens to me go on and on about him and she'll roll her eyes and say, "*Ya, cállate!*" which means "Enough already, shut up!" She doesn't understand why I think about my father so much. "It sounds like he's a real louse," Magda once said. "Besides, my *papi* always says you're like another daughter to him." I know Magda's trying to be nice, but I want to know my *own* father.

Three years ago, when Magda and I had confirmation

at the Catholic church, Tío Ricardo took us all out to dinner afterward. We went to a fancy steak house on Flatbush Avenue, where we sat at a long table in our own private dining room. I was having such a good time; I felt so special in my white dress. But when Tío Ricardo handed me and Magda identical tiny blue gift boxes, I almost cried. Each box was tied with a perfect white satin ribbon.

Magda opened hers in seconds, throwing the ribbon on the floor. Inside there was a gold cross hanging on a beautiful gold chain. *"Es oro, Papi,"* she said, giving him a kiss. *"Gracias."*

Magda is a true homegirl. For her, nothing is as good as gold. We were only in the fourth grade back then, but every day she wore thick gold-hoop earrings, a gold and coral bracelet, and three gold rings.

"Come on, slowpoke," Magda teased, pointing to my box. "Open yours."

I didn't want to open my box. I wanted to keep the present wrapped, so that I could make it a dream box— a box that could hold anything I ever wanted, or could imagine wanting. And what I really wanted was to pretend that my own father, not Tío Ricardo, was the one giving me a gift, wrapped in a box so blue that it looked like a little piece of sky.

Magda started tugging my arm, and everyone at the table was looking at me, waiting for me to open my gift.

When I pulled the necklace out of the box, it sparkled in my hand like gold dust. Even under the dim light of the restaurant, I could tell that it was real gold, not the *fantasía*, or fake gold, that they sell at the mall.

"Thank you, Tío Ricardo," I said, walking over to him and giving him a kiss.

He put one arm around me and one arm around Magda and he said, "I'm so proud of both of you, my little girls."

Now, sitting in the kitchen at the Rosarios', my hands red from grating yucca, I heard Tío Ricardo's deep voice, rolling up the stairs like an ocean wave.

"Luisa, are you trying to starve us?" he asked. "*Comida, Mami. Ahora.*"

Tía Luisa was, as usual, one step ahead of Tío Ricardo. She had already prepared a plate of *frituras* and was cutting open the coconuts and pouring the coconut water into a jug.

I carried the coconut water and the Panamanian white rum called Seco Herrerano down to the basement. Magda carried the plate of *frituras*. We made our way down the stairs carefully, so we wouldn't spill anything.

"*Ay, gracias!*" said all the men when they saw us coming. There were eight of them seated around an old card table. None of them wore jeans and T-shirts like American men. They were all dressed in pants that had been pressed, and they had on different colored shirts that glowed against the glistening sweat on their dark skin. The minute they saw the food and drink, they left their game of dominoes and started chowing down.

"*Mundial,*" Tío Ricardo said. "Fantastic. Tell Luisa to send more."

Magda and I laughed and ran back toward the kitchen, taking the stairs two at a time.

"*Mundial,*" Magda said, imitating Tío Ricardo perfectly.

"Yeah," I added. "He says to send more."

"More?" Tía Luisa said, casting a dirty look toward the basement door. "I've got twenty-five orders to fill for the morning and it's almost eleven o'clock. They better fill up on coconut water and Seco! Or they can come up here and cook for themselves. What do they think this is? A *fritura* factory?"

Mami and Luisa started laughing so hard they just couldn't stop.

"*Ay, manita,*" my mother said, wiping the tears from her eyes. "You're the worst." Then Mami and Tía Luisa started talking in Spanish, which they did whenever they didn't want me and Magda to understand. We can catch a few words here and there, but what Magda and I really spoke was Spanglish—a combination that was more English than Spanish.

"*Ay, manita,*" I said, putting my hand on my hip like

Mami does whenever she gets into gossip mode. "Let's speak in Spanish so our daughters don't understand."

"*Sí, mi amor,*" Magda said, following my lead and imitating her mother. "Let's get out of here."

Magda shares a room with her sister, Evelyn. I spread myself out on Magda's bed and she plunked down on the floor. God forbid Evelyn should have walked in and found either of us on her side of the room. Evelyn was in high school and was about to have her *quinceañera,* Sweet Fifteen, which is what they do in Latin America instead of Sweet Sixteen. *Quinceañera* is a big deal, almost like a wedding or a beauty pageant. You get to choose the girls to be in your court and the same number of guys to be escorts. Someone makes you a special dress, and all night you're the star. Evelyn already thought she was a movie star. But her *quince* was really taking her over the top.

"You know, Marisol, in two years we'll have our own *quinceañera,*" Magda said. It was June and we were both restless. That September we'd start eighth grade. Then after that, it would be high school and our *quinces.* For so long, it seemed like we would be kids forever. But now we were teenagers and everything was happening so fast.

Magda stood up and boldly sat at Evelyn's dressing table and began trying out different hairstyles.

"It's coming up so soon," I answered. "I don't know if Mami will have the money to pay for it. They cost a fortune."

"She'll find the money," Magda said. "She *has* to. Then again, you know Evelyn's friend Zuleika Ramirez? Her mother told her that if she didn't have a *quince,* she would give her the money to take a trip instead. She and her mom are going to Mexico for a vacation."

"Cool," I said. "I'd love to go somewhere far away."

Magda spun around in her chair. "Don't even think about it, Mayaguez!" she said, using my last name. "You've got to have a *quince.*"

Magda's forehead creased into little lines the way it always does when she's trying to figure something out. Then she jumped up with a big smile on her face and came over to the bed where I was sitting.

"I just had the best idea," she said, throwing her arm around my shoulder. "We could have our *quinceañera* together. Since your birthday's in May and mine is in April, we could have it sometime in between. It would save lots of money and be twice as much fun."

I didn't say a word.

"Isn't that the *best* idea?" Magda asked, her face bright with excitement.

I just smiled weakly, but Magda was too wrapped up in her ideas to notice the difference. She kept talking about her idea of a double *quinceañera*. Even though I didn't say anything, I hated the idea. The whole point of the *quince* was to have a night that was all about you.

I cracked my knuckles and turned the idea of a double *quince* over and over in my mind. There was no way I could go through with it. Magda could think what she liked, but I'd been dreaming about my *quince* my whole entire life. I dreamed of walking down a platform in a white chiffon dress, decorated with perfect Sleeping Beauty roses. Junior Vasquez would be my escort. The first song would be a slow dance and I would dance it so smoothly, not tripping even once in my brand-new high heels. Mami would be there and she'd be so proud of me. In my dreams, my father is there, too.

On that special night, no one would compliment me on being smart. They'd all say, "*Qué bella*; how lovely you look tonight, Marisol." I will have grown breasts by then. My twists will be down to my shoulders. In the tradition of the *quince*, I will be announced to the community of family and friends as a woman. When Junior Vasquez takes me out onto the dance floor, covered with ruby red petals, all eyes will be on me. Not Magda.

Magda was back at Evelyn's dressing table, trying on her sister's eye shadow. Somehow, I would figure out a way to tell her that I didn't want a double *quince*.

At least I had two years to do it.

2

"Marisol-Mariposa," I heard Mami calling. "*Vámonos. It's time to go.*"

"Ask your mother if you can spend the night," Magda said. We both ran down the stairs.

"Mami, can I stay over?" I asked, clasping my hands together like I was praying.

"Do you mind, Luisa?" Mami said, turning to Magda's mother. "You must be very tired."

Tía Luisa nodded in the direction of the basement where Tío Ricardo and his friends were laughing and arguing, the sound of dominoes slapping the table competing with the blaring rhythms of Tito Puente.

"Those *hombres* are more trouble than these *princesas*," Tía Luisa said, putting her arms around me and Magda.

"Okay, sweetheart," Mami said, kissing me on the forehead. "I'll see you tomorrow morning, first thing."

Tía Luisa took the car keys off the hook in the hallway. "I'm going to give Inez a ride home. I'll be back in a few minutes. "

Magda turned to me. "Come on, I'll show you the new dance that my brothers taught me."

"I'm not going to be able to do it," I said, trudging up the stairs.

Magda just laughed. "You *always* say that."

"That's because it's *always* true," I said, laughing along with her.

Magda turned to the rap station and started showing me the latest moves. I was almost getting the hang of it when we heard Magda's sister, Evelyn, coming up the stairs.

"Turn down that music, Magda!" she screamed. "I have a huge headache."

"She screams louder than the music," I whispered.

Magda just shook her head and turned the stereo off. "Let's get out of here," she said.

We went down to the kitchen and I sat at the kitchen table.

"In September, when we're eighth graders, we're going to rule Roberto Clemente Junior High," Magda said as she rummaged through the fridge. "You want a chocolate shake?"

"You know I do," I answered.

Magda took out the ice cream and chocolate syrup and started pouring it into the blender. Even though it was late at night, the Rosarios' house was alive with sounds. The dominoes game was long over, but downstairs Tío Ricardo was still talking to his friends. I could hear the hum of the upstairs television and I knew that Evelyn was watching a tape of the Spanish soap operas called *telenovelas*. José, Magda's oldest brother, was out on a date, but Rogelio, another brother, was steadily blasting rap tunes. Rogelio was just a year ahead of us in school. He and Magda fought constantly.

"Get lost," Magda sneered the minute she saw Rogelio come into the kitchen. "Me and Marisol are having a private conversation."

Rogelio was only fourteen, but at six feet tall, he made a super baseball player. "Talking about what?" he asked, making a face at me and then at Magda. He took the ice cream out of the freezer and began eating it straight from the carton.

"You are so *disgusting!*" Magda said. "You wait till I tell Mami about your nasty habits. Come on, Marisol, let's go get the sleeping bags."

I wasn't done with my shake, but I knew that Magda would be mad if I didn't follow her right away. I put my glass in the sink and when I turned around, Rogelio winked at me.

"Your twists are kinda cute, Mayaguez," he said, reaching out and touching my hair.

I just stood there for a second, cracking the knuckles on each hand.

Magda rolled her eyes and tugged my arm. "Come on, Marisol, it's getting late," she said. Then she turned to Rogelio and said, "Don't even *try* to rap to my friend, creep."

Walking down to the basement to get the sleeping bags, I wondered if Rogelio had really been hitting on me. Was there something cool I should have said? Evelyn, witch that she was, always had a quick comeback when guys tried to talk to her. But I wouldn't ask her for advice about guys. Especially not about her own brother. Not in a million years.

Magda and I rolled the sleeping bags out onto the living room floor. There was a pull-out bed in the sofa, but we liked to pretend that we were camping out.

"Let's paint our nails," Magda said. "I'll do yours and you can do mine."

"Okay," I said, even though Magda always smudged my nails when she did them.

She ran up to the bathroom and came back with a bottle of electric-blue nail polish.

"Cool color," I said, shaking the little bottle from side to side. Slowly and carefully, I began to paint Magda's nails.

"Marisol, I am just crazy about Stephen Cardoza," she said. Stephen was on the basketball team. He was tall and had the most beautifully colored caramel skin that I had ever seen. He was only fourteen, just a year older than us, but he already had the makings of a dark, silky mustache.

"So talk to him," I said. "You're never shy around guys."

"You don't understand. He's so good-looking, every time I see him, I just keep repeating myself. I say, 'Hi, Stephen. . . .' Then two seconds later, I say the same thing again, 'Hi, Stephen. . . .'"

I laughed. "Like you've ever been nervous around a guy, ever."

"I am," Magda insisted, her eyes were open wide in her sweet-and-innocent look.

"I bet you end up going out with him," I said, handing Magda the bottle of nail polish.

"These look really good," she answered as she blew softly on each nail. "If I went out with Stephen Cardoza, I'd be the happiest girl in the world."

"Then I'll keep my fingers crossed for you," I said. "Magda, do you really think Rogelio was hitting on me?"

"Do you *care*?" She sounded shocked, and the minute she said it, I regretted bringing it up. "He's a creep and a pervert. Besides, we're going to hook you up with Junior Vasquez."

Junior Vasquez lived in my building on the third floor. He was sixteen and gorgeous and a really good basketball player. He had never said more than "hi" and "bye" to me.

"Do you really think Junior Vasquez would go out with me?" I asked, my face getting hot.

"Sure," Marisol said, in her ultra-sure and grown-up voice. "No problem."

That's what I fell asleep thinking about: me and Junior Vasquez being no problem.

The next day was Saturday and everyone at the Rosarios' crowded into the kitchen to have breakfast. Baby Danilo was in his high chair, throwing cereal on the floor. José and Rogelio were at the kitchen table, devouring *carimañolas* and *tamales* in huge bites, as if they had teeth down their throat.

Both of Magda's older brothers played varsity sports— basketball in the winter, baseball in the spring. They were always talking about "carbo loading." Magda said that was just an excuse for them to hog the frituras, otherwise they would eat plain pasta like the other guys on the team.

Magda and I were eating *empanadas* and drinking orange juice while Tío Ricardo grilled us about American history. Tía Luisa stood at the bottom of the staircase, yelling for Evelyn to bring her *flaco* behind downstairs and eat with the rest of the family.

At our school it's a compliment to call someone *flaca*, or skinny. But not to Tía Luisa and all of Mami's Panamanian friends. In Panama, women are supposed to have hips and breasts, and as Mami says, "meat on their bones." Tía Luisa worried that Evelyn was too influenced by the American girls at school because she always seemed to be on one diet or another.

Finally, Evelyn stomped down the stairs and took a small container of yogurt from the fridge. "I'm eating this," she said to her mother. "Are you happy?"

Tía Luisa looked so mad, I thought she was going to knock Evelyn down on the spot.

"Dime," she said, grabbing Evelyn's arm. "Why isn't my food good enough for you?"

Tío Ricardo stood up and pulled Tía Luisa away. *"Deja, mi amor,"* he said. "Don't worry, Evelyn is fine."

Magda and I didn't say anything, but we gave each other our special look and headed for the door. We knew what was going on. Tío Ricardo always took Evelyn's side. We went into the living room to watch music videos and talk.

"Evelyn is a nightmare," Magda said. "But at least she doesn't make herself throw up like some of the girls at our school. If she did, I would know."

"How?" I asked.

Magda leaned in close as if she was about to tell me a really scary story.

"I would hear her getting up in the middle of the night to retch," Magda whispered. "You can smell it and after a while you can see it, because it makes your teeth rot."

"You're kidding," I said, trying to picture the glamorous Evelyn with rotting teeth.

"No, I'm not," Magda said seriously. As much as we ragged on Evelyn, I knew Magda really loved and admired her.

A few minutes later, the doorbell rang and I could hear my mother's voice in the hallway.

"Marisol," Tía Luisa called out. "Your mother's waiting for you. You have to be at your cousin's soon."

"Can I borrow that new mystery you've got?" I asked Magda.

"Sure," she said. "Come upstairs and get it. You know it takes me forever to finish a book."

"So what's going on at your cousin's?" Magda asked as I scanned her bookshelf for other books I might want to borrow.

"It's just a birthday party for my little cousin, Jason," I explained. "But you know the whole family will be there. Including Roxana."

"Not the T-Rex," Magda groaned.

The T-Rex was what we called Roxana because she was so tall. She was only fifteen, but she was already topping six feet. Magda had been to enough family gatherings with me to know how evil Roxana could be. She loved to tease us because Magda and I were *nacidas aquí*, or "born here." Roxana and all of my older cousins were born in Panama and spoke flawless Spanish. They thought they were so cool because they spoke Spanish and danced salsa better than I did. Roxana was the worst. She loved to use the fact that she had spent most of her life in Panama to kiss up to my mother and the other *tías*.

"Remember Miss Edith who lived in Colón. . . ." she would say. "Remember back in Panama when we . . ." Then she would launch into rapid-fire Spanish just to prove how Panamanian she really was.

"She's such a brown-noser," Magda said, rolling her eyes.

"I'll call you tonight and give you all the dirt," I promised as Magda walked me to the front door.

3

The party at Tía Alicia's was a kids' party, but the whole family came. It started with the kids in the afternoon, then went late into the night with the grown-ups dancing, singing, and eating. When Mami and I arrived, Tía Alicia greeted us with a big smile.

"*Hola, mi amor,*" she said, giving me a bear hug.

I liked the way Tía Alicia smelled like Mami, a sweet combination of Agua Florida and baby powder. Tía Alicia was dressed in a pink flowery dress and her hair was hot-pressed so that it was bone-straight. She looked just like a little doll. All of Mami's sisters—Tía Alicia, Tía China, and Tía Julia—are short like Mami, who's only five feet two. I'm already taller than all of them.

While Mami and Tía Alicia rambled on in Spanish, I glanced at my reflection in the hall mirror. My father had given me his height, if nothing else.

What good is it to be so tall, I wondered, looking myself up and down, if I can't reach the only thing I've ever really wanted—my *papi*?

I stood very still, thinking about Lucho.

"Are you okay, *niña*?" Tía Alicia asked.

"I'm fine," I said quietly.

Tía Alicia ran her fingers through my twists. "Your hair is getting so long. It's beautiful," she said. "Come to the kitchen and say hello to everybody."

In the kitchen the rest of the family was already busy at work. Mami unwrapped the plates of frituras she had bought, and everybody dove in.

"*De Luisa?*" Tía China asked, biting into an empanada. "*Qué sabrosa!* Delicious! Luisa's *frituras* are the very best."

Tía Julia, the oldest of my aunts, was at the sink cutting up fresh fruit for the punch. I walked up to her and gave her a kiss.

"Can I make the party bags?" I asked.

"So helpful!" Tía Julia said, grinning. "Just make sure the candy ends up in the party bags, and not in your stomach."

"I'll keep an eye on her," Tía China said, winking at me and following me to the table. Tía China had wild curly hair, and she always wore the hippest clothes and latest lipstick colors. She's my youngest aunt and my favorite.

We set all the treats into piles: Smarties, lollipops, Cracker Jack, and tiny plastic toys. We filled each bag with a little of everything.

"How are things, *niña?*" Tía China asked.

"Good," I answered, nibbling on a pack of Smarties. "Well, they *were* good until Magda told me that she wants to have a double *quince*."

Tía China made a face and pretended to choke herself. "Ugh," she said. "What a horrible idea."

I laughed. I didn't have to explain things to Tía China, she just *knew*.

"It's important for your *quince* to be your own," Tía China said, reaching out and covering my hand with hers. "The *quince* is the time when your family and friends honor and celebrate your passage into womanhood."

"Were you nervous during your *quince?*" I asked. "Walking into the ballroom wearing a long formal dress?"

"I was a little nervous," Tía China answered, unwrapping a Tootsie Roll. "But I felt like a princess. I'll never forget my *quince*. You won't forget yours either."

After we filled the last bag, Tía China jumped up and threw her arms in the air. "*Piñata* time!" she yelled, running toward the basement.

I raced down the stairs after her. In the basement Mami and Tía Julia were sitting on the sofa, sipping *café*.

Tía China stood on the stepladder, hanging the donkey-shaped piñata from the ceiling.

"Too high?" she asked me.

"No, just perfect," I told her.

Tía China stepped down the ladder and stared, disapprovingly, at the *piñata* hanging above us.

"You know, Marisol," she said, "In my day, we used to *make* our *piñatas*."

Mami let out a laugh that sounded more like a screech. "What?" Mami said. "*Your* day? You're only twenty-one years old."

"I know, I know," Tía China said as she picked up the shredded pieces of *piñata* paper that had fallen onto the floor. "But you know what they say in Panama."

We all turned to each other and said, in unison, *"Las cosas se hacen bien o no se hacen"*: Do things right or not at all. It was practically a family anthem with Mami and the *tías*.

The doorbell rang and I rushed to answer it.

"I'll get it!" I yelled as I bounded up the stairs.

"Hola!" I said, throwing the front door open.

It was Celia and Alfredo Molina and their four-year-old daughter, Kiki.

"Hola, Marisol," Celia said, pressing a red lipstick kiss

onto my cheek. "*Dichosos los ojos*, we haven't seen you in a long time! And where's your shadow?"

"Do you mean Magda?" I asked as we walked into the kitchen.

"Who else?" Alfredo said, squeezing my shoulder.

"She had to go to the dentist," I explained. "But Tía Luisa sent a whole bunch of *frituras*."

"*Frituras* from Luisa? I can't wait," Alfredo said, rubbing his hand across his stomach.

I felt a tug on my jeans and looked down. It was Kiki, trying to get my attention. She looked adorable. Her hair hung onto her shoulders in two perfect ponytails, and her yellow party dress was covered with little white ribbons. Every once in a while, I baby-sat for Kiki when Celia and Alfredo went out. She was one of my favorites.

"What's up, Kiki?" I asked, scooping her into my arms.

"Is there any candy?" she whispered into my ear.

"You know there is," I said, leading her down the stairs. "Let's find the birthday boy, he won't be far from the sweets."

Soon Mrs. Suarez arrived with her twins, Santo and Ramón. Felicidad and Mario Gomez showed up right after them. "*Compadres, qué tal?*" Felicidad called out from the top of the stairs. "*Mundial*, fabulous, couldn't be better," the aunts answered back.

Then Leticia and Mauricio Vega came with their son, Rafael. I'd have to keep an eye on him. Rafa was a little bully, and the last time we all got together, he had given Jason a black eye.

By four o'clock, the house was full. I was beginning to think that maybe Roxana wasn't coming, but I saw her slip in while Jason was opening his presents. I know she saw me, too, but luckily, she kept her distance. I wondered if she was getting bored with giving me a hard time, but I knew that was just wishful thinking.

I hated to admit it, but Roxana was very pretty. She had short curly hair, long eyelashes, and full lips that looked like they were drawn on her face. She was pretty, but she laughed like a horse.

"Marisol," Tía Julia said as I stared at Roxana across the room. "I want you to be in charge of the games for the little kids."

"I'd love to," I said, jumping to my feet.

First, I blindfolded Jason and his friends while they tried to hit the *piñata* with a baseball bat. Then, I stopped and started the cassette player during musical chairs. Before I knew it, it was eight o'clock and most of the little kids had gone home. Jason was upstairs sleeping, tired out from his long day.

The basement was now filled with grown-ups. All of the aunts and uncles were there as well as family friends.

Salsa music was booming from Tía Diego's stereo system and there wasn't a single person sitting down; everybody was dancing. I didn't know all the words, but I recognized the songs. My feet did a steady cha-cha to the rhythms of the *salseros*. At school dances it was tough to keep up with the pop and rap rhythms. As soon as I started to like a song or learn a new dance, it was out of style. Latin music was different. Even if the song was new, the basic beat was always the same. Tío Diego didn't buy many new albums. Most of his music was music I'd been hearing all my life.

Watching Mami and the *tías* rock to Diego's beats made me wonder what it would be like to have a sister, or two or three. Even though they all had husbands and boyfriends, they were so close. They were dancing in a circle, and Tía China was doing her best impression of Celia Cruz, the queen of Latin music. I stood in a corner, trying to mimic Mami's swiveling hips.

Next thing I knew, my cousin Roxana was hovering over me. She just stood there, laughing her horse laugh, and all my cousins turned around to see what was so funny. Why couldn't she mind her own business?

"Ay, Marisol. Why'd you stop?" Roxana said, faking an innocent voice.

"Stop what?" my cousin Manuel asked. He was sixteen and had a serious pimple problem that he just made worse by popping his zits constantly. Magda used to call him "Pepperoni Face," and I wished she was at the party to take my side. I was quickly being outnumbered by my own family.

"Marisol was showing us all a new dance," Roxana said, loud enough for everybody to hear her.

"For real," Manuel sneered, getting into the game. "Marisol, what's the dance called?"

Roxana started laughing again. "It's called the Pollo Loco—the Funky Chicken," she said, flapping her arms and turning around in a circle.

"*Bruja,*" I said. "You are such a witch."

"Ooo, I'm scared," she said, laughing her horse laugh. "You are so pathetic, *bailas como una gringa.* You dance like a white girl."

"And you laugh like *un caballo,*" I said, making a snorting sound. Manuel and my other cousins laughed, which made Roxana more mad.

"Get out of my face, Marisol," Roxana sneered, waving me away. "Take your *gringa* butt to the kitchen, leave the dancing to the true *panameños.*"

I rolled my eyes and walked away. I hated the way Roxana was always dissing me because I was born in the United States. At least I'd gotten her back. Even Manuel had laughed. I couldn't wait to tell Magda that I'd called Roxana a horse, to her face.

As I entered the kitchen the sweet smell of honey hit me right away. My mother and Tía Julia were making *sopapillas*.

"Can I help?" I asked, grabbing the spoon from the honey jar and licking it clean.

Tía China shooed me away. "We can lick our own spoons, thank you very much! Get lost, *m'ija*."

"But I can't go back out there," I explained. "Roxana is making fun of my dancing. Next thing you know she'll be making fun of my Spanish."

"Come on, Marisol," Mami said, passing me a plate with a hot *sopapilla*, honey oozing out of the side. "You mustn't be so sensitive."

"Come with me, *niña*," Tía China said, taking the plate out of my hand.

"Hey, I want to eat that," I said. "What's the big idea?"

"Later," Tía China said, grabbing my hand and leading me toward the living room. "I'm going to teach you how to salsa once and for all."

Tía China went over to Tío Eddie and requested a song. I knew what it was the minute I heard the rolling beats. Everybody went to the dance floor. I saw Roxana in the corner, flapping her arms and making fun of me. But holding Tía China's hand, I didn't care what Roxana did. I even started singing along. "W'appin', Colón!" I shouted with the rest of the crowd. "*Hola*, Panama!"

"Listen to me, Marisol," Tía China said, moving to the beat. "For salsa, you dance from the waist down. Don't worry so much about your arms. Shake your hips."

"But I don't have any hips, Tía China," I tried to explain, looking down at my bony body.

Tía China put her hands just below my waist. "You feel these two hard things?"

I put my hands where hers had been and felt the slight curve of my bones.

"That's where your hips *will be*," Tía China said, smiling. "But for now, *flaca*, my skinny girl, just shake your hipbones."

I shook my hips from side to side. I was afraid of looking stupid, but Tía China didn't seem to think I did.

"*Wepa*," she said, spinning around me. "You got it, girl."

Out of the corner of my eye, I could see Roxana standing in the corner. I just smiled at her and swung my hips in the opposite direction. I didn't care what she said or thought; I was salsa dancing. That night I called Magda. "Did you have any cavities?" I asked, even though I knew the answer. Magda was always eating candy and chewing gum and her mother always gave her a hard time about it.

"Only two," Magda said, and I could hear her

slurping on a lollipop. "Mami said *era un milagro*, the way I eat sugar. How was the party? Was it fun?" She wanted to know.

"Well, you know Roxana *had* to make fun of me."

Magda sucked her teeth, making a low hissing sound the way our mothers did when something bothered them.

"She thinks she's so cute," Magda said.

"I told her off," I said proudly.

"Way to go, Marisol!" Magda said. "What did you tell her?"

"I got right in her face and I called her a witch," I said. "But then I told her she laughed like a horse and *everybody* cracked up."

I snorted and made horse sounds over the phone.

"Really?" Marisol said, laughing. "You should have called her worse than that."

"And have my mother kill me? No thanks," I said. "Besides it turned out okay. Tía China gave me a salsa lesson and I think I'm getting the hang of it. I could show you."

"Salsa, ugh." Magda said. "I like rap much better. All the salsa songs sound the same. It's so old-fashioned."

"It's not so bad," I explained. "It's not like we could break out those moves at the school dance, but I'd like to get good enough to shut Roxana up forever."

"It'll take a muzzle to shut that girl up," Magda said.

"Definitely," I said. "Did you start on your Spanish homework? Those translations are a killer."

"I haven't even looked at it." Magda said. "What are you doing tomorrow?"

"Mami's taking me to the Museum of Modern Art. There's an exhibit of Latin American art. Want to come?"

"To the museum?" Magda made it sound like I'd asked her to come with me to the dentist. "I don't think so. I'll just meet up with you before school on Monday."

"At the handball court?"

"Sounds like a plan," Magda said. *"Hasta luego, mi mejor amiga."*

"See you later," I said.

4

On Monday I woke up, got ready for school, and poured myself a bowl of Frosted Flakes.

"You need something hot in your stomach, *niña*," Mami said, making her usual speech.

Mami always thought I needed to have something hot before I left the house in the morning: tea or porridge, preferably both. It didn't matter that it was June and it was already starting to get hot outside. Because Mami's from Panama, the weather in New York is never too hot for her.

I checked to make sure that I had my biology homework, then I kissed Mami on the cheek. But before I could make it out the door, Mami grabbed hold of my arm.

She looked me up and down. "Must you wear jeans every day, Marisol-Mariposa?" she asked. "You're turning into such a pretty young lady. Why don't you wear one of those nice summer dresses I bought for you?"

"Mami, come on," I pleaded. "I'm going to be late meeting Magda."

"When I went to school . . ." Mami began. And I knew exactly what she was going to say.

"When you went to school, all the girls wore dresses," I finished. "And George Washington was president. . . ."

"Very funny," Mami said as she laced up her white nurse's shoes. "Don't forget I have school tonight."

Mami worked as a nurse, but for the last year, she had been taking night courses. She was trying to earn a master's degree that would help her get a better job.

"See you later," I said, kissing her good-bye again. As soon as I got out the door, I started to run. I had to meet Magda at the school handball court. That's our spot. If Magda and I don't hook up in the morning, we won't get a chance to talk until lunchtime.

When I got to the court, Magda was playing handball with Tommy, a ninth grader in her brother Rogelio's class. I joined the group of kids watching her, and as usual, I admired Magda's game. You would think that because I was so much taller than she is, and skinnier, too, that I would have been the better athlete. But I wasn't.

Magda is short, strong, and fast. Her straight black hair flew like a flag in the wind as she dashed back and forth across the court. Tommy was huffing and puffing, barely managing to keep up with her.

"*Pa'alante*, Magda!" I yelled, happy to see her winning against a boy. "Give him fever!"

Magda turned around for a second and Tommy slammed the ball with his hand. Magda missed her return. Just then the school bell rang and everyone headed for the front door.

"What's up, girl?" I asked Magda as we walked toward our classes.

"I'm going to fix Tommy after school, that's what's up," Magda said, smiling. "I could beat him with my eyes closed."

"I know you can," I said. "I'll see you at lunchtime."

I walked into homeroom, just after the bell rang. Mrs. Park raised an eyebrow at me, but she didn't say anything. I liked Mrs. Park. She was young and wore all the latest styles. She also liked to tell jokes, ones that you had to be smart to figure out.

I spent most of my English and biology classes trying to sneak and write a letter to Junior Vasquez. My locker was full of letters that I wrote and never gave him. I had this never ending daydream about Junior. In it, I was in high school and Junior Vasquez was in college and he asked me out on a date.

"I've had a crush on you since I was thirteen," I

would tell him over dinner.

"No way," he would say, with a shocked look on his face.

"Yes," I would say, smiling and reaching out for his hand. "It's actually kind of funny. I think I still have a couple of the letters. I'll show them to you one day."

"Will you?" he would say, looking into my eyes. "I would love to see them. To think all this time, I had a crush on you and never knew you felt the same."

The lunch bell usually woke me from my daydream. And today was no exception. I ran down the stairs two at a time to meet Magda. But when I got to the cafeteria, I couldn't find her anywhere. She wasn't at our table. She wasn't in line. She wasn't even with the girls' basketball team, which is where we sometimes sat.

I was just about to sit by myself when I spotted Magda at a table full of boys, flirting with Stephen Cardoza. Magda was all smiles. She was wearing a deep burgundy lipstick that I recognized from Evelyn's dressing table. She reached over to Stephen and gave him a fake punch on the arm, then she smiled again. She didn't look nervous at all.

I walked up to the table where Magda and Stephen sat. "Yo, what's up?" I was trying to sound cool.

"Hey, Marisol," Magda said, not moving from her seat.

"Marisol, why don't you sit down with us?" Stephen said and gestured for one of his buddies to move over. The guy looked at me, and I could feel my face getting hot. I lowered my tray, careful not to spill it.

Steve asked me a few polite questions, but mostly he talked to Magda. That was fine with me. A table full of jocks left me tongue-tied.

When the bell rang, Magda said good-bye to Stephen and walked with me to my locker. The minute he was out of listening distance, she screamed.

"Do you believe it? I think he likes me."

"What happened to feeling like a dork around him?"

"I was *so* nervous sitting next to him," Magda screeched.

"It sure looked like it back there," I said, giving her a light shove. "Talk about a dork. I was doing my best impersonation of a silent-movie star. I didn't say a word all lunch period." I put my biology textbook in my locker and grabbed my Spanish book. Spanish was the only class that Magda and I had together.

"Come on," I said to Magda. She had popped open a compact and was going heavy duty with Evelyn's lipstick. "Did you finish those translations for Spanish class?"

"Oh, no! I was going to copy off of you over lunch," Magda said, putting her hand over her mouth. "But with

Stephen, I forgot all about it."

"Well, there's no time now. *Fue tremenda rompecabezas*, really hard."

"I hate Spanish," she said, dragging her feet.

"You hate Spanish. You hate salsa," I said, impersonating our mothers. "*Ay, niña,* what kind of Panamanian are you?"

"The American kind," Magda said, laughing.

I used to walk home from school with Magda; she used to live in my building. But it had been two years since she and her family had moved into the house on East Forty-first Street. Now she took the city bus home and I walked back from school alone.

I looked around the lobby of my building. The gray tile floor and the dirty white walls all seemed so plain to me. When Magda lived in the building, she would always cook up a great adventure. When it rained outside, we played spy games. The second floor where she lived would be Russia. My floor, the third floor, would be America. Junior Vasquez lived on the third floor, and back when Magda and I were eleven, we both had a crush on him. Magda made Junior's floor Switzerland. We always found an excuse to have peace talks in Switzerland.

I pressed the button for the elevator and looked

around the lobby. It was right here that Magda had taught me how to Rollerblade. I had been so scared of falling! I kept close to the wall, moving one hand, then moving one foot. But Magda was fearless. She would make up new tricks, scooting down on the Rollerblades then jumping in the air. Sometimes she fell flat on her face, but she didn't care. She twirled around and around with one foot in the air like an Olympic ice-skater or a prima ballerina. I missed having Magda live in the same building. When I was over at her house, it was always so lively. It felt like a home. Our apartment building just seemed dead without Magda. Mami was always at work or at school, and I was home by myself a lot.

I opened the door to our apartment, turning the keys of three locks. Then I locked each of the three locks behind me. It was warm and sunny in the apartment. I smiled to myself. Only two more weeks of school, and since I'd turned thirteen in May, this was going to be my first summer as a real teenager. I could hardly wait.

In the kitchen I made myself a peanut-butter-and-jelly sandwich, toasting the bread real dark the way I like it. Mami had school, which meant I was in charge of dinner.

On the stove there was a bag of chicken wings that Mami had taken out of the freezer before she'd left for work. I picked the yellow Post-it note off the bag and shook my head. I had been cooking for two years now, but Mami still felt the need to leave me Post-its all over the place.

I finished my sandwich, then turned on MTV, loud enough that I could hear it in the kitchen. I washed my hands, then put the chicken in a bowl to season it. Magda said uncooked meat made her sick. But I didn't mind. Sometimes I thought I should be a doctor because nothing grossed me out—not blood, not dissecting worms in biology, *nada*.

I took all the spices I would need off of Mami's rack— black pepper, garlic powder, bay leaves, oregano, basil, and, of course, Sazón Goya. I liked the way they felt in my hand and the way the whole concoction smelled when I was done.

I put the chicken in a pan in the oven, then I tried to call Magda, but she wasn't home. I watched a bunch of "I Love Lucy" reruns on Nickelodeon. At six o'clock I wandered over to the front window. Before Mami started going to school at night, I would always look out for her around six. As the sun began to set I saw all sorts of parents coming home from work. There were girls jumping double Dutch in front of the building, and Junior Vasquez was sitting on the steps with his homeboys. He was so cute. I sat watching him until he went inside. Would I ever be as brave as Magda? Would I ever tell Junior how I felt about him?

I sat down at the kitchen table to do my homework. Mami would have hated it if she knew I did my homework with music videos on, but I liked hearing the voices. It made me feel less alone.

After I finished my homework, I took a shower, put on my pajamas, and finished cooking. Then I sat down and served myself dinner. While I ate, I watched a documentary about sharks. Just when it was finishing, I heard Mami's key in the door.

She was wearing a white sweater, white leggings, and sneakers—her nurse's uniform. She had on a navy blue baseball jacket and a navy blue baseball cap over her short Afro. She looked young and beautiful. She also looked tired.

"*Hola*, sunshine," she said, giving me a hug.

"How was your day?" I asked, heating up her dinner in the microwave.

"Don't ask," she said, sitting at the dining table. "This chicken is delicious."

"It's the Sazón Goya," I said, smiling at the compliment. "Do you want me to put on a pot of tea for you?"

"No, hon," she said. "I'm going to sit up and study for a while. You go to sleep. You've done enough for today. Good night, Marisol-Mariposa."

Mami always calls me that. Mariposa means butterfly

and it's what Mami wanted to name me, but my *abuela* wouldn't let her.

"Your grandmother thought it was too much of a hippie name," Mami had told me.

I kissed her good night and went to sleep.

A few hours later, I woke to use the bathroom. The clock in the kitchen said four A.M. The dining room light was still on, and when I went in I saw that Mami was asleep at the table, her head on top of the books as if they were pillows. It wasn't the first time I had found her like this. Mami fell asleep while studying all the time these days.

"Come on, Mami," I said, shaking her softly. "You can't sleep here. You've got to go to bed."

She only seemed to be half awake as I walked her to her bedroom. "I'm so tired," she said as she crawled under the covers fully dressed.

"I know, Mami," I whispered softly, kissing her sleeping face. "I know."

5

It was the last day of school. I stood by the handball courts waiting for Magda. Standing by the fence, I tugged at the bottom of my shorts—they were a little shorter than I'd remembered. We were only allowed to wear shorts on the last day of school and I hadn't worn these since last summer. I looked at my watch; it was ten to eight. Where was Magda? She was never late.

All around me kids were screaming across the schoolyard as if they were long-lost friends. The arguments and differences that people had were squashed on the last day of school. Nobody wanted to leave for summer vacation with a grudge.

I couldn't wait for September. As eighth graders, Magda and I would rule Roberto Clemente Junior High. I had a feeling about this summer; good things were going to happen for me and Magda.

When I saw Magda walking toward me, I could tell something was wrong. Her shoulders slumped, and her eyes were trained on the sidewalk.

"What's up?" she said, still looking at the ground.

"What's up with *you?*" I asked. "It's the last day of school. You look like your dog just died."

"You can be so stupid, Mayaguez," Magda snapped. "How could you say something so cruel?"

"You don't even *have* a dog, Magda," I said, shaking my head. "What is bothering you?"

"Nothing," Magda said, biting her nails.

"Magda, I know something is wrong," I said, putting my arm around her. "I'm supposed to be your best friend. If you can't tell me, then who are you going to tell? Evelyn?"

"Marisol," she said. "I don't know how to say this, but you're moving to Panama."

"Yeah, right," I said. "And where are you moving? To the North Pole?"

Magda looked at me sadly. "I'm serious, Marisol, no kidding," she said softly.

The bell rang and everyone went rushing to the door. I sat down on the playground concrete, my back pressed against the handball court.

"We better go to class," Magda said. "I'll talk to you more at lunchtime."

"Don't go," I said, motioning for her to sit next to me. "You can't just drop news like that on me then take off."

Magda sat down next to me, and for a few moments, we didn't say anything.

Mrs. Croghan came over to where we were sitting. She had been my English teacher last year. "Girls, didn't you hear the bell?"

"Marisol isn't feeling so well," Magda said. "She has cramps. Can we just sit out here for a few minutes more?"

I clutched my stomach for effect, and Mrs. Croghan looked me over. "Okay, girls, I'll inform your homeroom teachers. But make sure you get to your first-period class on time, okay?"

We both nodded and I smiled weakly.

"It's going to be okay," Magda said, leaning to her left and pressing her head against mine. "We'll figure something out."

"Are you sure?" I asked, leaning closer to her.

"I'm sure," Magda whispered. But her voice was shaky, and she didn't sound sure at all.

It was a good thing it was the last day and we had no work, because I couldn't concentrate in any of my classes. I couldn't wait until lunchtime, when I could talk to Magda and figure out what was up.

When the lunch bell rang, I found Magda waiting for me by the door of my classroom.

"How're you doing?" she asked in a low voice, taking my hand.

"Not good," I said. "What's going on, Magda?"

"I heard my mother talking to your mother last night on the phone," Magda explained as we entered the cafeteria. "Your mother is worried that because she's in school, you're home alone too much. My mami offered to let you come stay with us, but your mother said no. She's already written to your *abuela*. She wants you to go to Panama."

We made our way through the lunch line. But I didn't take any of the food. I was too busy listening to Magda. Looking down at my empty tray, I reached for a plate of Jell-O that sat between cups of pudding and slices of cake.

I sat down at the table, letting Magda tell it all. Slowly, I opened the little plastic bag that held a spoon and a napkin, and I began to pick at my Jell-O.

"Why didn't you get a hamburger, Marisol?" Magda asked. "I know they're your favorite."

I just shook my head. "Magda, this is all so strange. Just this morning before you came, I was thinking about what a great summer it was going to be, you and me turning thirteen. I was thinking about next year, how we were going to try out for the drill team together."

Magda slid next to me on the cafeteria bench.

"You're my best friend, Marisol," she said. "I won't let you down. We'll figure something out."

"I hope so, Magda," I answered. "I really do."

That afternoon the minutes dragged by as I waited for Mami to come home from the hospital. I didn't have any homework to do; and all the music videos on MTV were the same ones I'd seen a thousand times. I sat in front of the TV, cracking my knuckles and checking the clock.

All I could think about was me moving to Panama. Was it true? Magda's Spanish wasn't good, maybe she just didn't understand what Tía Luisa was saying. Maybe Mami was just sending me on a vacation to Panama. I had so many questions, but only Mami could answer them. But she wasn't going to be home until six o'clock. I took three loads of laundry down to the basement and kept myself busy with that. I was sitting in the living room, folding towels and listening to my favorite rap station on the radio, when I heard Mami's key in the door.

"*Hola*, Marisol-Mariposa," Mami said, smiling.

"Hey," I answered softly.

Mami came into the living room and sat down in her

favorite seat—a lumpy blue chair that I had named the Cookie Monster.

"How was the last day of school?" Mami asked.

"Terrible, okay?" I snapped.

Mami took off her shoes and began massaging her feet. She looked over at me. "You're in a bad mood, *fea*," Mami teased, calling me ugly.

"I can't believe you're sending me away," I said finally.

Mami bit her bottom lip. She put both of her hands over her face and rested her head on the back of the chair. I knew then that Magda had been right. This wasn't a bad joke or a misunderstood piece of gossip. It was the truth.

Finally, after a long silence, Mami spoke.

"I don't have to guess where you got the news," she said, shaking her head. "I only received your grandmother's letter on Friday saying it was okay for you to come to Panama.

"This isn't the way I wanted you to find out, Marisol-Mariposa." Mami took a deep breath. "I wanted to take the time to tell you myself."

I could feel the hot tears in my eyes, and I fought to keep them from falling.

"What did I do so wrong that you would send me away?" The words were thick and heavy, like rocks stuck in my throat.

Mami shook her head. "Come sit on my lap."

I was taller than Mami and it had been *ages* since I'd done that. But I settled myself into her lap. My legs dangled over the side of the chair; it felt good to be so close to Mami.

"This is not a punishment," Mami said. "It's just that I worry about you so much, Marisol. It's too hard on you with my working and going to school. You're cooped up in the house, day and night."

"But I don't mind, Mami," I insisted.

Mami smiled then. "You never mind anything. You were such a good baby. You hardly ever cried at all."

"Mami," I said, rolling my eyes. "Quit with the baby stuff. I want to talk about what's going on right now. I don't want to go to Panama."

"Marisol, it's only for one year," Mami said, holding me closer. "It's going to take me forever to get my master's degree if I continue to take only one class a semester. I want to take a full course load in the fall and the spring; that way I can complete my program in a year. That means I'll be at school every night. All my weekends will be spent in the library."

"So now you don't have time for me," I said, folding my arms tight in front of me.

"Come on, Marisol, you're a big girl now," Mami said. "You know better than that. It's just that I want to finish school so I can get a better job and we can spend even more time together." I shifted in Mami's lap.

"*Ay, niña,*" she said. "You're heavy. My legs are all cramped."

Mami pulled me up and we stood facing each other.

"I love you, you know," she said.

"I love you, too."

She gave me a firm hug, and for the first time since I'd heard the news about going to Panama, I felt a little bit better.

Mami looked at her watch. It was almost eight. "Too late to start worrying about cooking now," she said. "Let's order in."

She went to the kitchen and opened the drawer where we kept all the take-out menus. "Chinese food or pizza?" she asked, holding two grease-stained menus.

"Chinese," I said, my mouth watering at the thought of shrimp-fried rice.

When our food arrived half an hour later, I was so hungry that I started to eat out of the paper cartons.

"Hello, Miss Slack," Mami said, using her thickest Panamanian accent. "In this house, we eat off of plates."

"But I'm so hungry," I said, not wanting to set the table.

"If you go down to Panama City with manners like that, Abuela will have a fit," Mami said. "She'll say I taught you nothing at all."

I rolled my eyes as I reached into the cupboard for the blue-and-white plates we used for every day. "Panama, *de nuevo, Mami*? Could we just not talk about it?" I asked, passing her two plates.

"Not talk about my country? That's my *patria* and you know how patriotic we Panamanians are," Mami said, trying to crack a joke.

"But, Mami, if I go to Panama, how will I talk to the people?" I asked. "Did you forget how bad my Spanish is?"

"Everyone in Panama speaks English," Mami said, serving herself chicken from the Chinese food carton. "You'll learn Spanish. You'll learn so many things."

"What if Abuela hates me?" I asked, shaking an extra packet of soy sauce onto my fried rice.

"There's too much salt in this," Mami said, taking the soy sauce out of my hand. "One packet is enough. And your grandmother *loves* you."

"But I've never even met her," I said "I don't *know* her and you're sending me to live with her for a whole year."

"You didn't know Tía China before she moved to the States," Mami said. "You didn't know Tía Alicia, and you love them."

"I also didn't know Roxana," I pointed out. "And I definitely *don't* love her."

"Marisol!" Mami scolded. "You do love your cousin. Don't let anybody hear you say different."

"When do you expect me to go?" I asked, shoveling a forkfull of food into my mouth.

"Two weeks," Mami said. "I don't want you sitting around here all day by yourself. The next semester of school in Panama starts at the end of July."

"What?" I almost choked. "You must be kidding. Mami, this isn't fair. This isn't fair at all."

I stood up from the table and charged into my room.

"Marisol!" Mami yelled. "Don't you dare stomp away from the dinner table."

I slammed the door of my room and waited for Mami to come after me. She had lots of rules, but the three major house rules were: No stomping. No temper tantrums. No slamming doors.

"Marisol, I know you are upset." Mami was standing at my closed door. "This isn't easy, I know."

I didn't say anything. I just looked down at the floor, tugging on the twists of my hair. I kept hoping that the blue carpet would open up, like Alice in Wonderland's rabbit hole. But it didn't. For me, there was no getting away.

"Marisol, you've got to work with me on this," Mami said sternly. "Please come back to the table and finish your dinner."

We finished eating in silence. I kept my eyes trained on the two *molas* that hung above the dining table. *Molas* are made by Panamanian Indians. They're strips of colored cloth sewn onto a black background in the shape of turtles and horses and fish. Mami had her *molas* framed in a beautiful light wood frame. I looked at the donkey and the turtle hanging above the table and wondered how many other things I would recognize when I got to Panama.

"You're from Panama, aren't you?" I asked the *molas* silently. "What's it all about?"

But the *molas* were stubborn and wouldn't speak. I guess I'll have to figure it out for myself, I thought as I scraped the last pieces of rice off of my plate.

After we finished eating, we washed the dishes. As usual, Mami washed and I dried. Mami kept going on and on about how great Panama was, when finally I asked her, "Mami, is my father in Panama?"

Mami took another deep breath and looked at me with tired eyes. "I don't know, *cariño*," she said sadly. "Nobody has seen or heard from him in years."

"I'd like to meet him," I said, hanging the dish towel on the hook beside the refrigerator.

"Ay, *niña*, why do you ask?" Mami said, shaking her head.

"Because he's my *father*," I said, my voice sounding

stronger and more sure than I ever remembered it.

"Marisol, there's something I want to show you," Mami said. "Come to my room."

I sat on Mami's bed as she pulled out her old photo albums. "I've seen these a *million* times," I groaned. It was the truth. Those old albums were full of people and places I didn't know or recognize.

"These pictures represent my whole life," Mami said, looking at each picture with a little smile. "Now these are places and people you'll see, *hija*. Panama won't be my *patria* alone. It will be something we can share."

Mami cupped my face with her hands, the way she used to do when I was little. Then she kissed me on my nose and on both my cheeks.

"Marisol, promise me that you won't go looking for your father," Mami said. "I understand your curiosity. But I know Lucho Mayaguez and he's no good. You would only be disappointed. He's a man with a lot of faults. He's just not the smiling person in that picture you keep."

I cracked my knuckles and looked down at the brown carpet.

"Put him out of your mind, *hija*," Mami said, taking my hands in hers. "This isn't about your father, Marisol. This is about you. It's about you growing up and going back to the place where your people are from."

"I don't want to leave here," I said, wrapping my arms around her. The minute the words came out, I could feel my eyes getting wet. "I'm so scared, Mami."

Mami sat back in her bed. Her hands clasped together as if she were praying. "Think of it as an adventure, Marisol," Mami said. "Like when you and Magda used to play spy games in the hall. Go be a spy in Panama for a year. And when you come back, you'll see how much you've grown. You'll have your own photo albums, *niña*. With or without your father, you'll have your own memories of Panama."

6

The next day I woke up with a start. The clock on my nightstand said ten o'clock.

"Oh, no!" I sat up in bed quickly. "I'm going to be late for school."

Then I remembered that school had let out for the summer.

On the dining room table, Mami had left me a note:

Marisol, querida,

I hope you slept well and are feeling better about going to Panama.

Tonight, when I get home from work, we'll call Abuela in Panama. Everything is going to turn out okay, Marisol-Mariposa. I promise you. I would never do anything to hurt you.

Love,

Mami

I took a shower and threw on an old pair of cutoffs and my favorite "Girls Rule" T-shirt. Magda had a T-shirt just like mine. We had bought them together at the previous summer's block party. Then I went into the kitchen and called Magda on the phone.

"Magda," I said, "you were right."

"I told you," she said. "Did you ask your *mami* if you could come and live with us?"

"She's not having it," I said as I poured myself a bowl of cereal.

"You can't go away, Marisol. Who will be my best friend?"

"Everything is not about *you*, Magda," I said quietly. "I'm the one who has to go to a strange country all by myself."

"I know, I know," Magda said. "I have to baby-sit Danilo. Do you want to come over?"

"Okay, I'll be there around three."

"Why so late, Marisol?"

"I just need some time to think," I told her, running my finger along the base of the phone.

"Suit yourself," Magda said. "I'll see you at three."

I slumped down on the kitchen floor with a bowl of Rice Krispies. When I was done, I put the cereal bowl in the sink. I walked into the living room and opened the window. I crawled out and sat on the fire escape. Mami would have killed me if she had caught me out there, but I didn't care.

It must have been a hundred degrees. I could feel the sweat under my arms and on my chest.

I looked out onto the street and tried to get used to the idea of leaving Brooklyn. Summer was the best time in the city. In the park the kids in my neighborhood played punchball. For lunch, Magda and I always ate spicy beef patties from the Jamaican store and washed them down with cool ginger beer, a Jamaican soda.

Someone had opened the fire hydrant down the block. It gushed a nonstop blast of water onto the street while kids tried to escape the water. They were screaming and giggling. I smiled, remembering when Magda and I used to do the same thing. We hadn't run through the hydrant since we were ten. Mami made us stop because she said we were getting to be young ladies and were too old to run around the neighborhood with wet T-shirts.

I closed my eyes and tried to imagine what Abuela's street in Panama was like, but I just couldn't. The photos in Mami's album were so old, they were pictures of a different world, a world that I couldn't imagine myself in.

I slipped back into our apartment, locking the window so that Mami wouldn't know that I'd been out on the fire escape. The apartment was so quiet, too quiet. I hit the button on the stereo and turned the music way up.

In my bedroom I pulled my twists back into a pony-tail. I stared at the pictures I had taped to the mirror on my dresser. There were a ton of pictures of me and Magda: when we were babies in a crib together, the first and last time that we looked alike; a picture of me and Magda riding the Cyclone at Coney Island; me and Magda in the shoe store when we had bought our first pair of heels for the school dance last year.

There was only one picture of my father. I carefully peeled the tape off the mirror and held the picture in my hand. It was a Polaroid that had been taken in the 1970s and had turned a weird shade of orange. Lucho, my *papi*, was standing in front of a convertible Cadillac. Mami was in the photo, too. She was so young, only seventeen, and she was wrapped in his arms. Mami hated the picture and was always telling me to throw it away.

"*Tírala en la basura,*" she would say, pointing to the garbage can.

But when she did, I knew she was only talking. She never expected me to trash the only piece of Papi I had.

I took down a picture of me and Mami, and I felt tears come to my eyes. In the picture I was wearing a beautiful white dress, satin and smooth, without all the little-girl ruffles Mami usually liked me to wear. I loved that dress. I'd been so happy that day.

The picture had been taken the previous Easter. In it, Mami and I were standing in front of the church. By that spring I was already as tall as Mami and we had our arms around each other. She was wearing a long purple skirt and a white silk blouse that glistened against her cocoa-brown skin.

I looked again at the photo of Lucho. What if I could go to Panama and find him? What would it be like to have two parents instead of one?

Once, I was watching a science program on TV. They were showing what happens when a person has a heart murmur. There was a big picture of a heart with the tiniest hole in it. The beating heart had the littlest bit of air escaping through its hole. It made the strangest sound— *boom-boom, sssshhhh. Boom-boom, sssshhhh*. That's how I felt about my father. Every time I thought about him, I felt a hole in my heart—a hole that let out air. I knew in that moment that I had to go to Panama. I had to try and find Lucho.

It was just a little before three o'clock when I rang Magda's doorbell. When I walked in, I was shocked at how quiet it was. "Where is everybody?" I asked.

"Rogelio is playing basketball and José is working,"

Magda explained. "I don't know where Evelyn is. I'm just glad she's not here."

In the living room Magda's little brother, Danilo, was playing on the floor with his favorite teddy bear.

"Hey, Danilo," I said, bending down to give him a kiss.

He started to drool and made a face that looked like he was trying to smile.

"He likes you," Magda said, grinning. "He knows you're part of the family."

"Thanks, Magda," I said, giving her a hug. "I'm sorry I hung up on you."

"No problem," Magda said. "Do you want an icey?"

Tía Luisa always kept a tray of iceys in the freezer. She poured all different kinds of juices into plastic containers and froze them on wooden sticks. They were Magda's and my favorite in the summertime.

"Yeah, that would be great," I said, sitting down on the couch.

"Watch Danilo," Magda said, "I'll be right back."

Danilo just stared at me. His huge brown eyes blinked only once every five seconds. I had always wanted a kid brother, but Mami hardly dated at all. I often wondered what it would be like to have a stepfather and brothers and sisters.

"Don't spill any on my mother's new couch. She'll

kill me," Magda said, handing me a piece of paper towel and a cherry icey. "So what are we going to do about this Panama thing?"

"Nothing," I said, shrugging my shoulders. "I'm going to go."

"Now you *want* to go?" Magda asked.

"No. Not really," I said. "It's just that I've been thinking. It's only for a year and well, maybe, I could find my papi."

"I get it," Magda said quietly. She never wanted to talk about my father. Magda and Tío Ricardo were so close, she didn't understand how hard it was for me not to have my own father.

"I'm so scared, Magda," I said, leaning my head on her shoulder. "You've got to know how hard this is. But Mami isn't changing her mind. And if there's a chance I could find my father, I should take it."

Danilo cooed. I sat down on the floor again and rubbed my hand over his wavy black hair. It was exactly like Magda's.

"Magda, you have to promise me that you won't mention anything about my father to anyone in your house," I said. "Mami doesn't want me to look for Lucho, but I can't go to Panama and not try."

"Are you kidding? Tía Inez can't stand your father!" Magda said.

"*Sucio*," Magda added, letting out a sigh and doing a perfect imitation of my mami.

"*Sinvergüenza!*" I said, crossing my eyes and sticking my tongue out. Magda and I burst out laughing.

"You can't blab about my secret, Magda," I said, serious again. "Finding my father means everything to me."

"I promise," Magda said, holding her golden cross in her hand.

I held my cross up too and Magda smiled.

"I hope you find him," she said, reaching for my hand and squeezing it.

I looked at our matching crosses, the way they hung on the delicate gold chains around our necks. I never took my *pequeña cruz* off because it was a constant reminder of why Magda was my best friend: I could trust her with my heart; Magda's promises were as good as gold.

7

That evening when Mami came home from work, we called Abuela. Mami doesn't call home to Panama very often because it's so expensive; we only talked to Abuela on Christmas and on her birthday. Whenever I had to talk to Abuela, I never stayed on the phone long. I never knew what to say.

I didn't really know any old people; Abuela is my only grandparent. When we talked on the phone, it was always the same thing:

"*Hola, querida,*" she would say. "How are you?"

"Fine," I answered.

"Are you keeping up your grades in school?" she usually asked.

"I am," I always told her.

Then she would say, "Stay sweet, *niña.* Put your *mami* on the phone." And I would.

Our conversation that night wasn't much different, except this time Abuela said, "I'm very glad that you're coming to Panama. I'm happy to have you."

Then Abuela and Mami talked on the phone for a long time, much longer than usual. Mami talked in Spanish the whole time. Not that I didn't know what they were talking about. She used my name in every other sentence.

"*Ay, la tristeza,*" I heard Mami say. "*Marisol estaba llorando toda la noche. . . .*"

"*Marisol es un angel,*" she said two seconds later.

Then it was, "*Marisol está nerviosa sobre su español. Pero yo le dije . . .*"

I could understand a little Spanish, but Mami was speaking so fast, I could barely keep up. I would have loved to speak Spanish as beautifully as Mami did. In my dreams I don't sound like a *nacida aquí*—a born-here American. In my dreams Spanish rolls off my tongue as smooth and round and colorful as a brand-new bag of marbles.

An hour later I heard Mami saying good-bye to Abuela.

"*Te amo, Mami.* I love you," I heard her say and when she came out of her room, I could see that she had been crying.

"I miss her so much," Mami said to me, as I prepared

for her a cup of *café con leche*. "We've been trying to get her to come to the States for years, but she's stubborn. She says in Panama she is independent, she has her life. She says she doesn't want to come here and be a burden. To tell the truth, I think that she wants to make sure she dies in Panama so she can be buried next to Papi."

"Is Abuela dying?" I asked. A vision of Abuela, all sick and frail, flashed through my head.

Mami waved her hand, as if pushing away the idea.

"Not even close," she said. "She's still a young woman. She's only sixty-six and in perfect health."

Only sixty-six didn't sound that young to me. "You kept mentioning my name," I said.

"I know," Mami said, holding my hand across the kitchen table. "She's very excited about having you. Apparently, there's a girl your age who lives in the apartment next door."

I hadn't thought much about what the kids in Panama City would be like. I was so busy adjusting to the whole idea of moving and thinking about my secret plan to find my father. But, of course, I had to go to school and a new school meant new kids. Who would be my best friend? Would Magda make a new best friend here?

The next two weeks were a whirlwind. There was so much to do before I left. Mami took me to the passport office to get my passport; all the aunts and cousins came over to visit. Everyone had something they wanted me to take to Abuela as well as advice and good wishes for me on my trip.

Things with Magda were so weird. I could feel her pulling away from me. She was always busy when I called, and she hardly came over anymore. I wanted to see her every day before I left, but she just wasn't interested. Mami told me that people handle separation in different ways, and that by ignoring me now, Magda was just trying to squash down the feeling that she would miss me so much when I was gone.

"It can't be easy for Magda," Mami had said. "Try to understand. She feels like she's being left behind."

"But *I'm* the one who's going away," I insisted. "To a place where I don't know anybody but Abuela, who I only know from pictures and the phone. I'm the one who everybody should be feeling sorry for."

"*Escúchame, niña,*" Mami said. "Listen up. You're going to Panama, my beloved homeland and the country of your heritage. You're not being sent to boot camp. There's no reason for anyone to feel sorry for you."

The Sunday before I was to leave, Tía Julia came over with Roxana. She brought me a going-away present—a suitcase covered with a beautiful rose print.

"You're a traveling woman, now," Tía Julia said. And while the suitcase was lovely, what made me even happier was to hear her call me *woman*. "*Gracias, Tía,*" I said, giving her a long kiss.

While Tía Julia and Mami talked in the kitchen, Roxana came into my room to torture me. She was sixteen and completely bossy.

"So what exactly do you intend to speak when you go to Panama?" Roxana asked. "I doubt any real Panamanians will understand that gibberish you and your little friend speak."

"Whatever," I muttered as I opened my new suitcase on the bed.

"In Panama, they speak *real* Spanish, not Spanglish, that cheap mix of Spanish and English," Roxana said, taking a nail file out of her purse and shaping her long nails.

"I'll manage," I said, trying to sound confident. "Don't worry about me, *prima*."

"I won't," she said, looking around my room. I was actually really proud of my room. Mami made the curtains in the room my favorite color: purple. The previous Christmas she had bought me a bedspread and a rug to match. I had decorated the room with pictures by my favorite artist, Frida Kahlo. Frida Kahlo was a Mexican woman who was really into her heritage and painted herself in all sorts of cool costumes.

Tía China had taken me to see an exhibit of her work in the city. Since then, I had begun to tear pictures of her out of art magazines and collected postcards of her paintings.

"This is kind of a cool room," Roxana admitted. "Maybe Tía Inez will let me stay here sometimes since you won't be around."

"You *can't* stay in my room!" I screamed. "You better *stay out* of my room."

I was so angry that I ran into the kitchen and jumped right in the middle of Mami's conversation. "She can't stay in my room," I said. "She can't." I looked over to the kitchen doorway, where Roxana was laughing that horsey laugh of hers.

"Marisol, pull yourself together," Mami said, and I could tell she was annoyed. "What are you talking about?"

"Roxana said she was going to stay in my room sometimes while I'm gone," I explained.

Mami and Tía Julia looked over to Roxana, but she just shrugged. "All I meant was that if I came to visit Tía Inez and it got late, maybe I could stay in Marisol's room while she was away."

"Roxana, you are sixteen years old and you're acting like you're younger than Marisol," Tía Julia said. She ran her hands through her short straight hair and then reached for her purse. She took out the car keys and handed them to Roxana.

"Do me a favor, child," she said. "Wait for me in the car."

"No problem," Roxana said, making a face at me. Then she asked Tía Julia how long she was going to be.

"*Hours*," Tía Julia said sarcastically.

But Tía Julia didn't stay for hours. She talked to Mami in Spanish for a few minutes, then she gave me a hug and a kiss.

"Roxana doesn't mean that we won't miss you," Tía Julia said. "Enjoy your present. I'll see you next week when I drive you to the airport. I'm very proud of you for taking this big trip without your *mami*." Then she headed for the door.

After she left, Mami and I went to her room to watch TV. We crawled under the covers and Mami started flipping channels.

"Why do you let Roxana get to you?" Mami asked as she fixed the twists in my hair that had come loose.

"I don't want to be replaced," I said in a quiet voice.

"I can't hear you," Mami said, pushing the mute button on the remote.

"I don't want to be replaced," I said a little louder.

"*Ay*, Marisol," Mami said, and I could hear how tired

she was by the raspy sound in her voice. "No one is replacing you, *niña*."

Although Mami had been extra sweet to me the last couple of weeks, I knew that she didn't really understand how scary all of this was for me.

"It's not just Roxana," I explained. "Magda is going to get a new best friend. I just know it."

Mami turned off the TV. The room was dark except for the candle glowing on her dresser. It was a tall white novena candle that Mami lit for *los santos*, the saints.

"Listen, *hija*," Mami said. "Magda is going to have to make new friends. But so will you. I know it doesn't seem like it now, but your friendship will only get better if you don't hold on to it for dear life.

"When I first came to this country my best friend, your Tía Luisa, got married and moved to California. She was a million miles away. But I made other friends, and the reason our friendship is so special now is because we allowed our friendship to change as our lives changed.

"Marisol," Mami said, putting her arms around me. "Loving people is not like buying something in a store. You don't have to choose one or the other. If you're lucky, you'll love many people in many different ways."

"Can I sleep in here tonight?" I asked, even though it had been ages since I had slept in Mami's room.

"Okay," she said. "But just for tonight."

As I fell asleep I thought about what Mami had said about loving different people in different ways. I considered all the people in Mami's life: how close she was to all my *tías*; and how even though the Rosarios weren't blood relatives, she treated each and every one of them like family. That night I realized that what makes Mami so special was that she had so much love, patience, and understanding to give to so many people.

I had no patience for people who were mean to me like Roxana was. To tell the truth, it wasn't exactly something I wanted to learn. I wondered if this impatience was a trait I got from my father. If the way he had walked out of Mami's life and never looked back was due in part to the fact that he thought he could love only one person at a time, that it had to be one or the other.

Was my *papi* a *sucio*, a good-for-nothing, because he replaced the people in his life with other people— keeping the passage to his heart small and narrow? I didn't know, but I hoped I would find out soon.

It rained all day on Saturday, the day before I was to leave for Panama. Mami came into my room to wake me up. We both sat on my bed, staring out the window.

"The city is crying because you're leaving," Mami said. It was silly, but it made me smile.

"I'm going to miss you so much," Mami said, giving me a tight hug.

"Me, too," I said.

"Marisol, *ya cantó el gallo*; it's time to get up," she said as she walked toward the door. "I'll make you a great big breakfast. We have a lot to do today to get you ready to go."

"No porridge. No tea," I called out.

Mami turned as if she was about to say something, then she just smiled and shook her head.

"Okay, *Princesa* Marisol, today's your day," Mami said,

pretending to bow before me. "One big bowl of sugar cereal coming up. A glass of orange juice, and maybe you'll eat an omelet?"

"An omelet's cool," I said, and got up out of bed.

I went to the dresser and looked again at the picture of Mami and my father. Only one more day and I would be in the same country as he was, the same city, maybe.

"*Te veo*, Papi," I whispered. "I'll see you soon."

I'd given Magda her space when she didn't want to hang out, but I couldn't leave Brooklyn without seeing her one last time or at least saying good-bye. I called Magda on the phone

"*Hola*, Tía Luisa," I said. "May I speak to Magda?"

When Magda came to the phone, her voice was flat. "What's up?" was all she said.

"Remember when we were little and we used to go Rollerblading in the rain?" I asked. "How about we go for one more spin?"

Magda was silent. Then softly she said, "Okay, I'll meet you at the playground."

I took out my Rollerblades and put on my old red raincoat and the goofy plastic hat that came with it, the hat I never wore.

Mami crossed her arms and shook her head when she saw me. "The last thing you need is to get sick the day before you leave," Mami said. "You're lucky I'm letting you go out in this weather."

"I thought I was *Princesa* Marisol and that this was *my* day," I said smiling.

"Don't push it," Mami said, giving me a pat on the back. "And be back before dark."

I laced up my Rollerblades in the lobby of our apartment building, then skated down the street. It felt good to be on wheels. Magda and I hardly ever went 'blading anymore. When we had first gotten the Rollerblades, we went out every day after school and all day on the weekends. But after a while, other things like punchball and shooting hoops took the place of 'blading.

When I got to the playground, Magda was turning figure eights. She was so graceful. Magda, who usually talked so much, was absolutely silent, skating like an angel.

"Yo, Magda," I called out to her.

"Hey, Marisol," she answered, not looking at me.

"Magda, I'm leaving tomorrow. Please stop icing me like this. We've got to talk."

I walked over to the swings and sat down. Magda skated around the jungle gym a few times before she joined me. The rain had softened to a drizzle, and the sun was starting to shine a little from behind the clouds.

"Magda, I can't believe the way you've treated me

the last couple of weeks; I'm going away and you've hardly spent any time with me at all."

"It's all about you, right?" Magda said. "All I hear in my house is that Marisol is going to Panama. 'How exciting.' 'What a wonderful experience.' Even Evelyn says it is cool that you are going down to the *patria*, getting to know your heritage."

I tried not to smile, but it did please me to hear that Evelyn, La Evil, actually had something good to say about me.

"Don't tell me that you're actually jealous that I'm being sent to Panama?" I asked, raising one eyebrow the way Tía China had taught me to do.

Magda didn't say anything. She ran her fingers along the metal chain of the swing.

"Maybe I'm a little jealous," Magda said finally.

"Look, Magda," I said, twisting around in my swing. "You're my best friend. *Punto*. That's all that matters. But this wasn't my idea, to go away like this. Mami didn't give me much of a choice, and now that I think I might actually find my father. . . ."

I stopped speaking and looked at Magda, noticing as I had so many times before that she had a heart-shaped face. It was like a valentine. Even when she was in a bad mood, her face was still a heart.

"I'm so scared, Magda," I said. "I'm going so far

away. Promise me that you'll always be my best friend. Promise me that you'll write. I can't go away thinking that our friendship is all twisted."

"It's not twisted," Magda said, giving me a hug. "We're cool. It's just that—"

"What?" I asked.

"I just hope that Panama is everything you want it to be, Marisol. What if you don't find your father? What if he's not a nice guy?"

"I'll deal," I said, running my Rollerblade along the edge of the playground fence.

"Will you write me?" Magda asked.

"You know I will," I said. "The question is, will you write me?"

"I'll write," she said. "I promise. You know you're always going to be my girl."

"Mejores amigas," I said, giving her a soul handshake, fist on top of fist, just like the homeboys do.

"Best friends, forever," she said, smiling. *"Mejores amigas, siempre."*

That night, I couldn't sleep. It was like the night before Christmas. I was nervous and jittery and excited all night long. In the morning, Mami ran around the house, adding more things to the heavy bags and suitcases that I had already packed.

"Take another toothpaste," she said. "You never know. And I think you should take a towel. That way, if Abuela doesn't have an extra, she won't have to spend money to buy one." It seemed to me that Abuela would have towels, but I didn't argue.

I placed the suitcase Tía Julia had given me on top of my bed. It was packed with all my personal favorite things. My diary. My teddy bear. My pictures of Mami, Magda, Tía Luisa, and Tía China. I tucked the picture of my father into the knapsack I would be carrying onto the plane.

"Be good," Mami said as we sat down to our last meal together—my favorite *empanadas*, *arroz con pollo*, *plátanos*. "Don't give Abuela a hard time. Write me every week, and I'll call when I can. But don't feel bad if I don't call every day, because you know it's so expensive."

I just nodded. Mami had been saying the same things for weeks.

"*No te preocupes, Mami,*" I said, holding her hand. "Don't worry. I'll be fine."

Then Mami started to cry. She got up to hug me and I could feel her tears, warm and wet, traveling down my cheek and onto my shoulder. It wasn't long before I was crying, too.

"I only have one daughter," Mami said, putting her

hands on my shoulders and squeezing hard. "You've got to take care of yourself because you're all I have."

"I know, Mami," I said, hugging her tighter. "I know."

The doorbell rang and I heard Tía Julia call out, *"Soy yo,"* over the intercom. I buzzed her into the building. When Mami opened our front door, Tía Julia took one look at her and said, *"Ay,* already the tears have started!" She smiled and held Mami close. "It's okay, *niña. No te preocupes."*

"Things are so expensive in Panama City now," Mami said as we loaded all the bags and suitcases into Tía Julia's car. "Whatever we can send will help a lot."

When I looked at all the stuff, I felt like a pack rat, because all the *tías* had things they wanted me to take for Abuela and different friends in Panama.

Mami sat in the front seat while Tía Julia drove over to the Rosarios'. When Tía Julia honked her horn, Magda and Tía Luisa came running out. They were coming with us to the airport. When Magda got in next to me, we immediately grabbed hands.

"I'm so nervous," I said.

"I don't want you to go," said Magda.

Mami turned around and squeezed my knee, then Magda's. "I know you're going to miss each other."

A few minutes passed and it was like neither Magda nor I knew what to do or say. Then Magda said, "Let's play red car, blue car."

"Okay," I agreed.

Red car, blue car is a game Magda and I would play when we were little kids. She counted all the red cars and I counted all the blue cars. Whoever saw the most cars in their color would win.

"Red car," Magda called out, her face pressed to the windowpane. "Red car, red car."

"Blue car," I called out. But I wasn't really paying attention to the game. I kept thinking about Panama, my abuela, my father."

I sat back in the seat, staring at my hands and cracking my knuckles.

Magda kept saying, "Red car! Red car!" Then she turned to me, "Hey, Marisol, you've missed *eight* blue cars."

I didn't say anything, I just kept cracking my knuckles.

Tía Luisa ran her fingers through my twists and squeezed my shoulder. "Magda, I think Marisol just needs some quiet time."

"Are you okay?" Magda reached for my hand.

"It feels so weird that this time, I'm the one who's leaving. . . ."

In our family, Mami and Tía Julia had been the first to move to America and get their green cards. Then they sent for the other *tías* and my cousins, one by one. I used to love going to the airport to meet the relatives from Panama. The flights always arrived at night because everyone worked during the day. Tía Julia would come and get me and Mami in her car. Because none of the cousins ever wanted to go, I would have the backseat to myself on the ride to the airport.

When I was little, I loved to lie across the backseat and pretend that Tía Julia's car was a navy blue rocket. I would pretend that I was an astronaut shooting into space. Out the window, the lights on the Brooklyn–Queens Expressway twinkled like stars against a night sky. Stretched out in the back, I would pretend that I was floating in space.

In the backseat with Magda next to me and Tía Luisa sitting on the other side, I was surprised at how little had changed. Outside, the expressway lights still looked like stars. I wasn't pretending to be an astronaut, but I still felt like I was shooting in space.

Mami, Tía Julia, and Tía Luisa kept going back and forth in Spanish and English—speaking Spanish between themselves, speaking English when they were talking to me and Magda. I didn't say much. It seemed like my mouth wouldn't form the things I really wanted to say: *I love you. Don't forget me. Miss me as much as I will miss you.*

At the airport Tía Julia parked the car, and we all piled out. When Mami checked my luggage, she explained to the airline attendant that I was traveling alone. Then we got to a place in the airport with a sign that said: TICKETED PASSENGERS ONLY BEYOND THIS POINT. I knew then that I was on my way, that there was no turning back. I said good-bye to Mami and Tía Julia and Tía Luisa. They kept pressing back my hair, covering my face with kisses.

Finally, it was time to say good-bye to Magda. I hugged her, and when I did, I heard her little gold cross touch mine. It was the softest sound in the world, and it echoed again and again inside my heart.

It was the sound of our sisterhood, and it rang as clear and true as a bell.

9

When the plane landed on the runway, the lights of Panama City glittered bright against the night sky. My heart was beating fast and furious. As I waited for my turn to get off the plane I kept whispering to myself, "I'm here. I'm here. I'm here."

When I walked into the airport building, the first thing I felt was the heat. In New York, it was hot, but it was city heat. You could feel how the heat was packed in between the buildings, the way it bounced off the concrete and all of the cars. Here there was space all around; the heat seemed to move like waves through the open air. I couldn't see the ocean, but I knew that it was near. I could smell what Mami and all the Panamanians we know call "sea air." There were palm trees with leaves that rustled like music. It was quiet in Panama, much quieter than in New York.

When I got to the gate, I saw Abuela right away. She was like a picture come to life, standing alone, apart from the waiting crowd of people. And she was so tiny! Just like Mami and all my tías. I was taller than my own grandmother.

"*Buenas noches, Abuela!*" I said, approaching her.

"*Querida,*" Abuela said, grabbing me in a big hug. This was the first time I was meeting Abuela, but everything about her was familiar. She had Tía China's smile. She had straight, dark hair like Tía Julia. She smelled just like Mami did when Mami got out of the shower—a mixture of hair grease, baby powder, and Agua Florida cologne. And the pink flowery dress that she wore must have been a present from Tía Alicia. In Abuela's arms, I felt safe.

Abuela found a porter to help us carry the bags and suitcases I had brought with me. We stood at the taxi stand, outside of the airport, and I tried to see out to the city beyond us. This strange place was going to be my home.

The apartment building where Abuela lived was so much smaller than our building in New York. Our building at home had six stories and one hundred apartments. Abuela's building was only two stories high, with four apartments on each floor. Abuela lived on the first floor.

All the furniture in Abuela's apartment was so old. I recognized it from the pictures Mami had. It was also the neatest, cleanest apartment I had ever seen. Immediately, I thought of Tía China and Mami saying: *"Las cosas se hacen bien o no se hacen."* Do things right or not at all. I could see that Abuela was not going to mess around with the chores. There wasn't a single speck of dust or anything out of place.

Glancing around the tiny living room, I didn't understand how everything could be so different and yet still feel so familiar. The brightly colored *molas* with their double wooden frames were just like the ones Mami and all the *tías* had back in New York. I ran my fingers along the tea-colored doilies. They too were just like the kind Mami had.

"Would you like a piece of bun and some tea?" Abuela asked.

"Yes," I said, remembering how hungry I was. I'd slept through the meal on the plane.

I sat down at the kitchen table with Abuela and sipped on my tea.

"Don't slouch," she said in English. "I hear you're very Americanized. But in my house children act like children."

I looked away from Abuela and started cracking my knuckles. Who was she calling a child? I was thirteen years old. I was about to begin eighth grade. At home, Mami was always working or at school, and while I couldn't go outside and play, I didn't have anybody bossing me around. With Abuela retired and home all day, she'll be hanging over my head with rules and chores, I thought to myself.

"*Niña*, I know that you've had to take on a lot of responsibilities with your *mami* so busy," she said. "You think that you're just meeting me for the first time. But I know you, Marisol-Mariposa."

I just peered down into my tea. What did she mean, she knew me?

Abuela moved her chair closer to mine and reached out for one of my hands. Her hand was so wrinkled, I expected it to feel hard and scratchy, but it didn't. Abuela's hand, her skin so soft and caramel brown, felt as if it was covered in a cashmere glove.

"When I say that in my house, children must act like children," Abuela explained, "I mean that I want you to relax and enjoy being a child. Your mother has written to me about all you have done for her while she attends school. But I can clean my own house and I'll cook all the meals. The only thing I'll expect you to do is to keep your room clean and make your bed."

Abuela got up then and poured us each a fresh cup of tea.

"*Ay, niña,* if only you knew how your mother worries about you," she said as she sat down.

I thought about Mami and how much I missed her, and I started to cry. I tried to hold back the tears, but I couldn't.

"I didn't mind Mami working so hard with her job and school," I said. "I never minded any of it."

I looked up at Abuela, who placed her hand on my shoulder.

"I didn't want to come here," I admitted. "When Mami first told me about sending me here, I threw a fit."

I didn't tell Abuela what had made me change my mind. If Mami didn't want me to find Papi, Abuela wouldn't want me to look for him either.

"Why don't you get some rest," Abuela said. "You must be tired. And tomorrow we're having lots of company for breakfast. There are many people who want to meet you."

"There are?" I asked, following Abuela to the back of the apartment.

"You know, this used to be your cousin Roxana's room," Abuela said, turning on the lights of a small room with bright yellow walls.

Before I could stop myself, a groan had escaped my lips. I was hoping to forget all about Roxana during my time in Panama.

"*Qué te pasa?*" Abuela asked, trying to read the expression on my face.

"Let's just say that Roxana and I don't get along," I answered, putting my floral suitcase on the bed and taking out my favorite teddy bear.

"*De veras . . .*" Abuela said, smiling. "Because you remind me of Roxana when she was your age."

"No way," I said, folding my arms tightly in front of me.

"She was already so tall, just like you," Abuela said. "And she was fresh, quick to talk back, as I can see you are."

"*I'm* not fresh," I said sweetly.

"Yes, you are," Abuela said as she walked out of the room. "But I don't mind. I raised all my girls to be outspoken. It's important for a woman to be able to speak her mind. Enough for now. Get some rest. *Buenas noches.*"

I sat unpacking my suitcase and thinking about what Abuela had said. She was definitely *un poco tiesa*, a tough cookie, but I didn't mind. Like Abuela, I preferred women who were fresh.

After Abuela went to bed, I reached into my orange knapsack and took out the picture of my father. Abuela didn't know it, but I planned on finding Lucho Mayaguez before I left Panama.

Back in Brooklyn, I'd had countless dreams about what would happen when I met my father and what I would say to him.

I would speak to him in Spanish, of course, a Spanish

so flawless he would never realize that I had grown up in the United States. He would be surprised to have such a grown-up daughter, and I would speak to him, not as a little girl, but with the poise of a young woman.

"*Mucho gusto, Papi.* I am very pleased to meet you," I would say, offering him my hand to shake and speaking to him with respect.

He would kiss my hand like a gentleman, then hold me in a tight hug.

"I have been looking for you for years," he would say, tears filling his eyes. "I knew that you would never forget me."

"No, Papi," I would say as I held his hand in mine. "I have never forgotten you."

In the morning I woke up with a jump. *This isn't my bed*, I thought, looking around. *This isn't my room.* Then I remembered where I was and felt the homesickness sitting in a tight ball at the bottom of my stomach. I was in Panama with Abuela. I liked Abuela already, but I missed Mami and Magda and everyone at home.

I sat up in bed and was about to call out to Abuela when I heard a bunch of voices coming from the kitchen. I looked at the clock next to my bed. It said seven o'clock. *What's going on out there?* I wondered.

There was no one in the living room, but the kitchen

was full of people. Abuela, dressed in a light blue sleeve-less dress and a beautiful gold necklace, was sitting at the table, holding court like a queen.

Abuela's kitchen was tiny, but there must have been fifteen people all squeezed together in there. And everybody was talking at the same time.

"*Buenos días.*"

"*Cómo está?*"

"*Mírela . . .*"

"*Allí está.*"

One of my worst nightmares about living in Panama had come true. A bunch of strangers speaking rapid-fire Spanish as if I could understand it all, as if I knew enough Spanish to answer them back. I smiled and nodded, hoping nobody would notice how confused I was.

"*Al fin*—finally," Abuela said. "Sleeping Beauty awakens." I could've kissed Abuela's feet for turning the conversation back to English.

"We've been waiting for you for over an hour," Abuela explained. "We've already had breakfast, but there's tea and *frituras* on the stove.

I stood next to Abuela, trying not to be too obvious. "Who are all these people?" I whispered.

"These are our neighbors and friends," Abuela said, gesturing to the people across the room. "They've come to meet you."

I walked over to the sink and picked up a clean cup off the counter. Outside the tiny kitchen window, the sun was already shining. The leaves on the trees were greener and shinier than any I had ever seen, as if God had polished them himself.

It's so beautiful here, I told myself. I wish Magda could see it. I touched my gold cross and wondered what Magda was doing right then, and if she was missing me as much as I missed her.

As I began eating breakfast, I noticed a girl in the group who looked as if she might be around my age. She must be the girl that Mami mentioned, I thought, remembering what Mami had said about Abuela's next door neighbor being in my grade.

She looked over at me and smiled. I smiled back. I wanted to talk to her, to ask her about the school and what kids in Panama did for fun, but I never got the chance. I was surrounded by the women in the group, every one of whom had something to tell me.

Their skins ranged in tone from cream-colored to the deepest ebony. Some of the women had straightened hair like Tía Julia and some of them wore their hair curly and wild like Tía China. They all reminded me, in one way or another, of my *tías* back home. They spoke to me in English and without bothering to introduce themselves, they talked as if they'd known me forever.

"You've grown so much," a tall woman in a blue dress said, patting me on the head.

"My name is Gloria," said one woman who reached right out and hugged me. "Your mother and I have been friends since we were *your* age."

"I've seen so many pictures of you," explained Gloria. She reminded me of Tía Julia. She had the same little wrinkles around her eyes when she smiled. Gloria reached for the straw bag on the counter and took out a school picture of me from when I was in the third grade.

I looked at the picture and couldn't believe it. I was wearing a goofy plaid jumper and my hair was done in six plaits, like Martian antennae, sticking out all over my head.

"*Where* did you get this?" I asked.

"Inez, your *mami*, sent it to me," Gloria explained. It was weird. Mami never told me that she sent my school photos to people in Panama.

"My name is Clara. Your mother and I went to school together," said a woman who, like Mami, was very small with a short, curly Afro. Then she brought over the girl that I had been eyeing.

"This is my daughter, Ana," Clara said. "We live next door."

I know that if Magda saw Ana, she would burst out laughing at Ana's clothes. Ana wore a bright pink sundress with orange-tinted glasses and orange sandals. The look was a little kooky, but I liked it.

"*Hola, mi nombre es Ana. Soy tu vecina. Vamos a pasar mucho tiempo juntas. . . .*"

Ana spoke only in Spanish, so fast that I needed more than a translator, I needed a traffic cop. I stared at her for a long minute.

"*No hablas español?*" she asked me.

"*Sí, hablo español.* Yes, I speak Spanish," I said. "But if you could speak a little slower . . ."

Everyone in the kitchen laughed. Abuela reached out and patted Ana's arm. "They don't call Ana 'Speedy Gonzales' for nothing," she said.

"Don't worry, I speak English, too," Ana said, hooking her arm into mine. "I've *always* wanted an American friend. Stick with me. I'll show you around. You're going to be in my class at school. We're going to have so much fun."

"*Espero que sí,*" I said, following Ana into the living room. "I hope you're right."

10

The next morning Abuela woke me up early. "We have to go to the market," she said, shaking me gently. "We don't have all day."

"*Abuela, please,*" I begged. "Five more minutes."

"Forget about it," she said, flipping on the lights and turning on the clock radio full blast. "I hope you like pancakes."

I sat up in the bed, groggy but hungry. "With blueberries?" I asked.

"You're in Panama," Abuela said, laughing. "Bananas or coconut?"

Banana pancakes? Coconut pancakes? They both sounded pretty strange. "Can I get them mixed together?" I asked.

"Definitely," she said. "Now don't take all day in the shower."

I picked up the neatly folded pink towel that Abuela had laid on my bed.

"You know, Mami was worried that you might be too poor to have an extra towel," I said.

"I can afford extra towels," Abuela said, waving her hand as if to dismiss the idea. "My retirement check isn't much, but I manage."

"Why don't you move to America?" I asked. "You could live with me and Mami."

"Why don't you move to Panama?" Abuela asked, placing her hand on her hip.

"I just *did*," I reminded her.

Abuela didn't say anything at first. She looked at me with a faraway look in her eye, then she nodded her head.

"I guess that's true," she said, smiling. "Now, don't be all day in the shower."

My banana-coconut pancakes were delicious, the best I'd ever had. And by eight o'clock Abuela and I were out the door. The market wasn't a grocery store as I had imagined it to be. It was more like a street fair, with people selling everything from spices to fruit and rice from stalls. Walking past the different *vendedores* selling their wares, I wondered if they could tell I was American. I was dressed in my favorite pair of jeans and my "Girls

Rule" T-shirt. Most of the other girls I saw wore brightly colored sundresses, like the one Ana had worn the day before.

When we stopped to buy rice or fruit, the vendors always greeted me in Spanish and expected me to understand. I did, for the most part, but I was still nervous about trying to use my Spanish. So when people spoke to me, I nodded and smiled.

"You're going to have to speak Spanish at some point," Abuela said. I was surprised that she had noticed that I wasn't talking.

"La única manera de mejorarse es practicando," Abuela said, taking my hand and leading me down another row of *vendedores.* "The only way you'll get better is to practice."

"You don't understand," I said. "At home people make fun of my Spanish."

"People?" Abuela asked, raising one eyebrow. "People like who?"

"Like Roxana and my friend Magda's brothers and sister."

"No importa," Abuela said. "It doesn't matter now. You'll be speaking like a native in no time at all. That is, if you speak. You've got to open your mouth and try."

We passed a stall where a woman was selling homemade cookies. "Can I have some?" I asked Abuela.

She just looked at me. "I don't know," she said. "Ask her."

I walked up to the woman's table and spoke slowly. *"Buenos días, señora."*

The lady smiled and asked me what I wanted. *"Buenos días, niña. Qué quieres?"*

"Quiero dos galletes de chocolate," I said. "I want two chocolate cookies."

Just then, I felt a finger poke me in the back. *"No dices por favor?"* Abuela said.

"Please," I added.

The woman smiled again and handed me the cookies in a little plastic bag. Abuela paid, I thanked her, and we walked away.

"You spoke Spanish and no one laughed," Abuela said, raising her left eyebrow.

"No one laughed," I said, taking a bite of a cookie.

Two weeks later Abuela registered me for school. It was the first week of August and I couldn't help but feel that my summer vacation had been cut in half. At the school, Abuela and I met the guidance counselor, a woman named Mrs. Ortiz. She was beautiful—tall and dark-skinned with wavy shoulder-length hair, like Tía China.

"All of your teachers speak English," Mrs. Ortiz explained. "They'll give you as much help as you need."

I looked at the printed schedule she had handed me. I was taking Spanish, English literature, and math in the morning. Then science, history, gym, and art in the afternoon.

"Well, I think you're all set," Abuela said, standing up. "Make sure to meet Ana to walk home from school."

"Bye, Abuela," I said, smiling.

"This is really a terrific opportunity for you," Mrs. Ortiz said as we walked to my first class. "Immersion is the best way to learn a language. Maybe you could tutor one of the students in English, and the student could tutor you in Spanish. I'll talk to your homeroom teacher, Señora Baptiste, about setting something up."

I started cracking my knuckles as soon as I walked into my homeroom class with Mrs. Ortiz. Standing in front of a classroom of total strangers was not my idea of a good time.

"Class, I want you to meet Marisol Mayaguez," Señora Baptiste said.

It was strange hearing how Panamanian my name sounded, when I didn't feel Panamanian at all. I stared down at a square on the floor.

"You'll be fine," Mrs. Ortiz said. *"No te preocupes."*

At lunchtime I walked into the cafeteria. I just couldn't stop cracking my knuckles. It was the most knuckle cracking I'd ever done and my fingers were starting to hurt. Then I saw Ana, waving to me.

"Marisol, *ven acá*," Ana said. "I saved you a place at my table."

I was relieved that I wouldn't have to sit alone, but afraid to sit at a table where all the kids spoke nothing but Spanish.

Ana was wearing a blue sundress with white flowers all over it, the same orange sandals, and the same orange-tinted sunglasses.

"*Estás de moda, Ana,*" I said. "You look great."

"Thanks," she said, standing up and giving a little spin. "I guess I'm stylish enough for America."

I wasn't sure about that, but I didn't say anything. Ana was my only chance at a new friend so far. I wasn't going to hurt her feelings by telling her that the girls I knew in New York would never wear an outfit like hers.

After school I met Ana, and we walked home together.

"Tell me all about Nueva York," Ana said as we walked down the tiny winding street. "Do you know how lucky you are to come from New York, the Big Apple? *Wow!*"

"Well, nobody *in* New York calls it the 'Big Apple,'" I said, laughing.

"Do you go to clubs every night?" Ana asked, talking

as fast in English as she did in Spanish. "Do you meet lots of rock stars and famous people?"

"As if," I said, jumping down a hopscotch drawn on the sidewalk. At least some things were the same in Panama.

"*As if*," Ana repeated. "*Que significa* as if?"

"It means 'no way,'" I explained.

"So what do you do for fun?" Ana asked.

"Me and my best friend, Magda, we watch music videos and play punchball in the park," I said, shrugging. "Just regular stuff."

"Your regular stuff sounds *muy divertido* to me," Ana said.

"Do you have a best friend?" I asked as we crossed the street. I knew where I was now. Abuela's apartment building was at the end of the block.

Ana scratched her arm and looked down. "I did have a best friend," she said quietly. "Her name was Digna. But she's not here anymore. She moved to Nicaragua to live with her father. I had to start the school year completely by myself."

I thought about Magda in New York. We were going to take Roberto Clemente Junior High School by storm this year—drill team, honor roll, everything. Now I was here starting the school year completely by myself and Magda was there—in New York, without me.

"I'm glad you came to Panama," Ana said, opening the door to her apartment.

"Thanks, Ana," I said. I stood on the porch for a second. Looking out onto Panama City, the palm trees blowing in the wind.

I thought about the scene in the *Wizard of Oz* when Dorothy says, "We're not in Kansas anymore, Toto." That was exactly how I felt, and I didn't even have a dog to tell it to. I was in this on my own.

"Cómo te fue hoy?" Abuela asked, wiping her hands on her apron. "How'd it go today?"

"Not bad," I said, trying to smile. "Not bad at all."

"Okay, we'll talk over *cena*," she said. "You go and relax."

I kept thinking about what Mrs. Ortiz had said, about how coming to Panama was an opportunity. She had said the best way to learn a language was through "immersion." It was a funny word—immersion. I kind of knew what it meant, but I had never heard anybody actually use the word in regular conversation.

I went into the living room, to the shelf where Abuela kept all her books. I pulled out the *American Heritage Dictionary* that I had spotted a few days before. I opened it and was surprised to see my mother's maiden name, Inez Velásquez, written in her same perfect handwriting.

This dictionary must have belonged to Mami when

she was in school, I thought, and even though it was just a book, I held it to my chest for a second.

I sat on Abuela's old red couch, the couch filled with stuffing that had popped out on the side. I opened the dictionary and flipped to the *I*'s. The word was listed under its root word—*immerse*. The definition read: IMMERSE—1. TO PLUNGE INTO A FLUID. 2. TO BAPTIZE BY SUBMERGING IN WATER. 3. TO ABSORB, ENGROSS.

I thought about what I had been doing the previous summer, at exactly this time. I was in New York, and Tío Ricardo, Magda's father, was teaching Magda and me how to swim at the Y. He insisted that all we had to do was jump into the cold water. Every day, he waited for us on the deep side of the pool and held out his arms as we plunged in. He let us struggle for a second, then pulled us up out of the water. Eventually, we stopped struggling and started to float.

Holding Mami's dictionary open on my lap, I closed my eyes and remembered how dark it had been underneath the water, how the pool water burned going up my nose, how the chlorine stung my eyes. Magda had been her usual fearless self, but I was so scared.

Sitting in Abuela's living room, I remembered when my arms and legs began to move in sync. It wasn't more than a dog paddle, but it was the first time that I actually didn't sink like a stone.

Panama—the language, the place, the people—was like that pool, only deeper and wider.

There were oceans that now separated me from everything and everyone I'd ever known. But Tío Ricardo had taught me that it was the body's natural instinct to float.

"Don't fight so hard to swim, *hija*," he had said when I splashed and splashed like my life depended on it.

"It'll come naturally," he said.

Now I was *immersed* again, plunged into this place that everyone in my family called home.

"I've jumped in. Tío Ricardo always said that's the hardest part," I whispered to myself as I put the dictionary back on the shelf. "Now let's see if I can swim."

11

When I heard the pounding on the front door, I knew exactly who it was.

It had been a week since I'd started school and Ana and I already had a routine down pat. She picked me up at Abuela's in the morning and I waited for her on the side steps of the school in the afternoon.

"I've come to pick up Marisol for school," I heard Ana say.

I was in the bathroom trying to pin my twists up. I poked my head into the living room. "*Que pasa, Ana?* You're early," I said.

"I know. I just couldn't wait for our usual time, so Mami said I might as well come over," Ana said cheerfully as she sat down on Abuela's couch.

Standing in front of the bathroom, I stared at myself in the mirror. I touched my necklace and little gold cross and thought about Magda. This would be the first year, in seven years of school, that we didn't meet by the handball courts before class. I had already written her three letters, but I hadn't gotten a single one back from her. I was worried. I wanted to pick up the phone and just call her, like I used to. But I knew that I couldn't. It was way too expensive and I couldn't do that to Abuela.

That morning in homeroom Señora Baptiste introduced me to Rubén. He was a tall boy with shoulder-length dreadlocks and honey-colored skin. He was cute, or as Magda would say *"fine."* I had noticed him, on my first day of school, in my English class.

"Marisol, I want you to meet Rubén," Señora Baptiste said. "He's going to be your Spanish tutor. Rubén is an excellent English speaker. So from now until the end of the semester, you two will meet in the library during your second-period English class. He will help you with your Spanish, and once you're up to speed with that, you will help him with his English."

"Hi," Rubén said, smiling broadly.

"*Hola*," I said, answering him in Spanish.

Señora Baptiste patted me on the back. "Very good, Marisol. We want you to speak Spanish as much as possible. Believe me, with Rubén's help, you'll be fluent in no time."

When the bell rang, Rubén said, "I'll see you second period," and I took off for my algebra class.

When the second-period bell rang, my heart started to race. All through math class, I couldn't stop thinking about Rubén, about how his dreads framed his face and how much I had liked his smile. I rushed over to the library, then made myself count to three before going in so I wouldn't seem too anxious.

"What's up?" I said, joining Rubén at a large round table in the corner of the library.

"No, no, no," Rubén clucked, mimicking Señora Baptiste's prissy voice perfectly. "*En español, por favor.* In Spanish, please."

I smiled. "*Buenos días, Rubén,*" I said. "*Qué pasa?*"

"Not much," Rubén said, answering me in English.

"I thought we were supposed to talk in Spanish," I reminded him.

"*You're* supposed to speak in Spanish and I'm supposed to speak in English," he said.

"What fun," I said sarcastically. "You'll be talking to yourself because my Spanish is *muy malo.*"

"Come on, it's not that bad," Rubén said. "If you want, we'll start in English. But if a teacher comes in, we've got to go to Spanish. Open your Spanish textbook, just in case."

I reached into my knapsack and grabbed my old Spanish book. Back home, I'd been in the top class for Spanish. But the book we used in New York was considered so basic here in Panama, it was used to teach grammar to seven-year-olds. It was embarrasing to have people see me with it, but I followed Rubén's instructions and opened it.

"So where are you from? California?" Rubén asked hopefully.

"Are you kidding?" I said, rolling my eyes. But when I took a look at his baggy Jams pants and his Internet T-shirt, as well as the baseball cap that he fastened onto his belt loop. I could read his vibe in two and a half seconds.

"Let's see, you asked about California and you've got a totally alternative rock fashion thing going on," I said, still checking him out. "Let me guess, you're a surfer boy?"

"Good guess," Rubén said, smiling. "So have you ever gone surfing?" Rubén asked.

"Do I *look* like I go surfing?" I asked.

"You're American," Rubén said. "I thought all American teenagers loved to surf."

I stared at him for a second and wondered if he was kidding.

"Well, for one thing," I said. "Most of the people who surf are white and blond and live in California."

"That's not true here," Rubén said. "Maybe it's because there aren't that many white, blond people."

"The fact is," I explained to Rubén, "*no one* surfs in New York."

"But I looked at the map," Rubén said. "The Atlantic Ocean is right there."

I wondered if Rubén was stupid or just clueless.

"Just because the ocean's there doesn't mean you can surf in it," I tried to explain.

"Why?" he asked.

"I don't know why," I admitted. "You just don't."

I looked around the library at all the books on the shelf behind Rubén and the bright colorful posters that hung on every wall. I used to love going to my school library back home. But here, everything was in Spanish: all the posters, all the directory information, all the books.

"I feel so stupid," I said to Rubén. "I bet I couldn't read one single book in this library."

"That's what I'm here for," Rubén said. "*Hay que practicar.* You have to practice."

"How did you learn to speak English so good?" I asked, doodling in my notebook.

"Cable TV," Rubén said, totally serious.

This time, I couldn't help myself, I burst out laughing. "No way," I said.

"Sure," Rubén said. "MTV, CNN, ESPN, Nick at Night.

"Did you ever watch Spanish TV in New York?" Rubén asked.

"Not really." I shrugged. "My best friend's sister used to watch *telenovelas*. . . ."

"Oh, those are so bad," Rubén said, rolling his eyes. "I can't believe they show those in the United States."

"Oh, yeah," I said. "They show lots of them."

We sat there for a moment, smiling at each other, and all I could think was, I wish Magda could see me now, talking to a fine guy like it was nothing at all.

After school I waited for Ana in our usual spot, under the shade of a huge palm tree near the side steps of the school building.

"I am *totally* in love," I said, grabbing Ana's arm as we walked home.

"With who?" Ana asked excitedly.

"This guy named Rubén," I said. "He's so cu—"

"He is *really* cute," Ana said, cutting me off. "And he's super nice. I had three classes with him last year. He used to hang out with my best friend Digna's brother, so I would see him at their house all the time."

We were walking by a little tree with red flowers

when Ana stopped and asked, "Do you want to see a trick?"

"Sure," I said.

She plucked a flower, then bent down and rubbed it into my leather sandals. My shoes looked all cleaned up when she was done.

"It's a hybrid tree," Ana said. "It's like nature's shoeshine. "

I smiled. "My friends in New York would never believe this."

We walked a little farther and I wondered how I could bring the conversation back to Rubén.

"Hey, Ana," I said. "Do you think a guy like Rubén would like me?"

"Are you kidding?" Ana said, and I just stood still. Was she going to diss me? Had I been stupid to think a cool guy like that would like a girl like me?

"You're the totally cool American exchange student," Ana said. "He'd be lucky to go out with a girl like you."

I stared at her in disbelief. Is this what the other kids thought of me? Could I really be the totally cool anything? I didn't know what to say.

"Qué chévere," I said, using Ana's favorite expression. "Unbelievable."

That night, I wrote Magda a letter.

Dear Magda,

No vas a creer esto. *I mean you really won't believe it. I'm not in love with Junior Vasquez anymore. I've met an extra-fine Panamanian guy named Rubén. Would you believe that* este muchacho guapo *has been assigned to be my tutor? That means I have to spend forty-five minutes alone with him, every day.* Qué lástima, eh? *What a shame. Well, don't cry for me, Argentina!*

The girl next door, Ana, is pretty cool. I'm sure I told you about her in my last letter. I feel really bad for her because I just found out that her best friend, a girl named Digna, moved to Nicaragua last year, right before they were going to start the eighth grade together. Remind you of anyone? Pero somos dichosas, *at least, I'm coming back. Ana's friend, Digna, is gone for good.*

Ya te olvidaste de mí? *Magda, you haven't answered any of my letters. Stop being such a cretin and write me back, okay?*

I M-I-S-S you.
Your best friend,
Marisol

P.S. Ana said that Rubén would definitely go out with me because I'm the "totally cool American exchange student." Me? As if.

12

Mami called me and Abuela every Friday night. Because it was so expensive, she only stayed on the phone for ten minutes. She would talk to me for five minutes or so, and it was never long enough.

"How are you?" she asked me. Three weeks had gone by and while I wasn't totally used to Panama, I was getting by.

"*Muy bien*. I'm good," I said. "*Me gusta mucho mi vecina, Ana*. I like hanging out with Ana a lot."

"Good," Mami said. "And I can see that your Spanish is really improving."

"You sound tired," I told her.

"I am," she said, her voice dropping, as if even talking was too much effort.

"New York's not the same without mi *niña*," Mami said. "Now let me talk to your *abuela*."

"Okay, hold on," I said. "I love you, Mami."

"I love you, too, Marisol-Mariposa," Mami answered.

Mami and Abuela talked for a few minutes, then Abuela said good-bye, too.

"I miss her," I said to Abuela as I sat down to our evening snack.

"Me, too," Abuela said, sipping her *café*. "It's been thirteen years since I've laid eyes on my daughter Inez."

I knew it had been a long time, I just didn't know how long. "I'm glad you came to Panama, Marisol," Abuela said, holding my face in her hands, the way Mami sometimes did. "Family should be together."

That night, before I went to sleep, I took out the picture of my father. I wondered what pictures Abuela kept hidden away. I thought about how she must miss Mami and the *tías*, and if she felt that little hole in her heart that I sometimes did. It was strange. It had never occurred to me that I wasn't the only person in this apartment who was missing someone.

That Saturday I woke up with a craving for pancakes.

"Can we have banana-coconut pancakes for breakfast?" I asked.

"*Claro que sí,*" Abuela said. It was nice having Abuela at home all day. She made me breakfast every morning before I left for school, and she was home when I came back from school. Between Ana and Abuela, I always had company. I liked it, but it didn't mean I'd stopped missing Mami.

After breakfast Abuela took me swimming.

"You can swim, can't you?" she asked.

"Yeah," I told her. "Tío Ricardo taught me and Magda last summer at the Y."

I went into my bedroom and put on my swimsuit. It was navy blue with white stripes on either side. I loved the way it crisscrossed in the back. Magda had one just like it. We had bought them together the previous spring.

When Abuela came into the living room, I couldn't believe how old-fashioned her bathing suit was. It had a little skirt and little cap sleeves. It was more like a dress than a bathing suit.

"What did you expect?" Abuela said, smiling. "A bikini?"

We put on our clothes over our suits and headed toward the bus stop. On the ride down to the beach, Abuela told me stories about Mami and Tía Luisa when they were my age.

"Those girls lived at the beach. They were practically mermaids. I used to call them *mis sirenas*," Abuela said.

The bus stopped and a young couple got on. They walked to the back of the bus, holding hands.

Abuela looked over at them, then continued her

story. "I remember when Luisa first started going around with that boy, Ricardo."

It was strange hearing Abuela call Magda's dad "that boy, Ricardo." I wished Magda was around to listen to all of Abuela's great stories.

"That boy, Ricardo, would come to our house and eat everything in sight," Abuela said. *"Que apetito tenía Ricardo."*

"When Tía Luisa makes *frituras* on Friday night," I told Abuela, "she sends down a big plate to Tío Ricardo and his friends. They *always* ask for more."

"Hmm," Abuela said, nodding. "See, *no me sorprende.*"

Abuela signaled the bus driver to stop, and when we got off the bus, we stood at the top of the beach. It was unlike any beach I had ever seen before. The sand was clean, and the ocean was so clear that it seemed more like a painting or a mirage than something you could actually go into.

"This is so beautiful," I said. "It sure beats Coney Island."

"I should hope so. The ocean is our pride here. *Mira qué bella son las aguas de Pánama.* Look at how beautiful it is," Abuela said, admiring the view. "Let's find somewhere to sit."

When Abuela had picked the perfect spot, we laid our towels side by side.

I was afraid to ask, but I knew that I had to.

"What do you remember about my father, Abuela?"

"What do I remember?" Abuela said, putting her hand on her hip. "I'm not senile. I remember everything. When your father first came to my door, asking to speak to your mother, she was only sixteen years old.

"Inez was too young to date in my opinion, but I said okay. Those girls probably tell you stories about how strict I was, but really, I let them get away with a lot."

I was too tall to fit onto much of my towel—Abuela's towels were tiny—so I lay down sideways, my legs in the sand.

"Can I put my head on your lap?" I asked.

"*Sí, niña*," Abuela said, continuing with her story. "Once it got started, you couldn't see Inez without seeing Lucho.

"He used to live in the Wilcox Building, and he'd come over at all hours of the night, knocking on the door. One night I heard Lucho calling 'Inez, Inez' from the bottom of the stairs. I'd just finished mopping, so I took the bucket of dirty water and dumped it on his head."

"You didn't!" I said, my eyes opening at the thought of Lucho soaked with dirty water.

"*Por atrevido,*" Abuela said. "I had to teach that boy some manners. You don't call my daughter from the street, like she works a corner. You come and knock on the door, *como un caballero*.

"*Hace tanto calor*," Abuela said. "Let's go into the water and cool off."

I followed her silently down to the water's edge. But my thoughts were with my *mami* and *papi* and their teenage love.

After we had finished swimming and dried ourselves off, Abuela asked me if I wanted to see where she bought her seafood.

"Sure," I said, rubbing my stomach. "I love fish."

"Let's walk this way," Abuela said, leading me down the beach in the opposite direction of the bus stop. We walked farther and farther until Abuela spotted a group of women standing at the edge of the beach.

"That's it." Abuela pointed to the group of women.

I turned and saw that the women were waiting for a large boat that was slowly heading for the shoreline.

"You mean you buy your fish straight off the boat?" I asked, wrinkling my nose.

"Can you think of a better place?" Abuela asked, putting one hand on her hip.

"Yeah," I said. "'The store. It's cleaner there."

"It's *fresher* here," Abuela said, tilting her head toward the ocean.

We turned around and started walking toward the bus stop.

"Do you know what *Pánama* means?" Abuela asked.

"There isn't a meaning," I said. "It's just a name like Brooklyn. "

Abuela shook her head. "Everything has a meaning. Even if you don't know what it is. *Pánama* means 'abundancia de peces,' an abundance of fishes."

We walked for a few minutes in silence, our eyes mesmerized by the crashing waves.

"Mami never talks about my father, you know," I told Abuela.

Abuela paused for a second, twisting her mouth sideways the way she did when something got on her nerves.

"You have to understand," Abuela said. "Inez was so hurt. She thought when Lucho married her, that it meant he would stick around. But then he ran away. I told her she was better off without Lucho, but she didn't want to hear that. She was twenty-two, she'd had you, and she was living in New York, so far away from home. But it's like I always say, *mejor sola que mal acompañada*."

I never thought about Mami that way, being so young and heartbroken. No wonder she called my father *sucio* and got upset whenever someone mentioned his name.

"Have you seen him?" I asked, wondering if I should

tell Abuela about my secret hope of finding my father.

Abuela just shook her head. "No, *niña*. Lucho knows that if he were to show up at my house, I'd throw more than dirty water at him. *Dejemos el pasado en paz*. Don't think about him. Come on, let's go for a swim."

I followed Abuela down to the water's edge. Every man who looked to be about Mami's age, playing Frisbee with a little kid, sipping a cold beer with his friends, caught my eye. I was going to find my father. I wouldn't tell Abuela about my plan, but for me, the past wasn't past. Last year, in honors English, I wrote a poem that reminded me of my father. It went like this:

An ocean separates us,
but my heart swims across.

I miss mi papi, Lucho,
he's always in my thoughts. . . .
My love for him could never be lost.

13

I had been in Panama for two whole months when I decided to tell Ana about my father. We were in the cafeteria, having lunch, when I took Lucho's picture out of my knapsack.

"This is my *papi*," I said. "He's somewhere in Panama—maybe even here in Panama City. Will you help me find him?"

Ana took the picture from my hand and studied it carefully. Back in New York, Magda was never really interested in my father. She listened to me go on and on, but I don't think she ever looked at his picture the way Ana was doing now.

"He's a very handsome man," Ana said finally. She passed the picture back to me. "You look like him."

"*Gracias*," I said, "I guess I inherited some of his looks."

"Is this the only picture you have of him?" Ana asked. I nodded yes.

"That might be tough," she said, "He may look very different now."

"I know, but I can't imagine what he might look like now," I said, taking a bite of my *jamón con queso* sandwich. "For me, he's always been the man in the picture."

"When was the last time you saw him?" Ana asked.

"I was a baby, so I guess you could say I've never met him at all," I explained. "Which is why I have to find him, Ana. Without him, there's a part of my heart that's missing.

"One more thing," I said. "You can't tell my *abuela*. You can't tell your parents either."

"It's a promise," Ana said, making the sign of the cross over the lime green T-shirt she was wearing.

Then Ana turned to a piece of paper in one of her notebooks, and at the top of the page, wrote CLUES in giant letters.

"Okay, Detective Mayaguez," Ana said. "What do we know about the case so far?"

"Ana, come on," I said, shaking my head. "This is really serious."

"That's why I'm writing it all down," Ana said. "We have to be very organized."

"Okay," I said, "His name is Lucho Mayaguez. The

other day Abuela said that he used to live in the Wilcox Building on Ninth Street. But that was years ago, before I was born. It seems to me, if he was still there, Abuela would have seen him around the city."

"Maybe not," Ana said. "Here's what we'll do. I'll pick you up on Saturday and we tell your *abuela* that we're going to the park. Instead, we'll head over to the Wilcox Building. Maybe someone there remembers him or maybe he left a forwarding address."

"Or . . ." I whispered to myself, *"maybe, he'll be there."*

After school the next day, Abuela and I went to the post office to check the mail. I had been checking every other day, and there hadn't been a single letter from Magda in over a month. But when the man at the post office handed Abuela a pink envelope with scented stickers all over it, I knew that my luck had changed.

"That one's for me, Abuela," I said, reaching out for the letter. I turned to walk away when I heard the post-master call out to me.

"Marisol Constancia Mayaguez?" he asked.

"Yes." I turned back around.

"You have a package slip as well." He went into the back of the post office and returned with a big box.

"You're a popular girl today," Abuela said, adjusting the strap on my pink sundress.

When the postmaster handed me my package, it took me less than two seconds to recognize the careful, neat handwriting on the box.

"De Mami!" I said, grinning at Abuela.

On the way home Abuela carried the box while I ripped open Magda's letter. It was September, and Magda had just started school:

Dear Marisol,

I can't believe what a terrible summer I've had. All I did was baby-sit Danilo and listen to Evelyn run her mouth. Stephen Cardoza went to basketball camp, so I didn't get to see him even once. He did write me four letters, though. He's like you—a much better writer than I am.

School started last week and I don't know what to think yet. Before we found out that you were going to Panama, I had been so psyched to start the eighth grade. We were going to rule *Roberto Clemente Junior High, remember? Well, I have news for you, it's cool to be an eighth grader. But you can't rule a school without your best friend.*

Drill team tryouts are next week and you'll never believe who's been helping me learn the routine. La Evil—my sister, Evelyn. She says she doesn't want to see me embarrass the family name by not making the team. I think she just feels sorry for me because my summer really sucked without you.

This boy, Rubén, sounds cute. Does he have a brother? A twin brother? One that lives in New York? I'm just kidding (sort of).

Any luck finding you know who? Write me as soon as you know anything.

Still your best friend,
(even though you moved away)
Magda

At home Abuela put the box from Mami on the dining table and before you could count to ten, I was trying to peel back all the tape with a pair of scissors. But Mami had taped the box up so tight.

"*Ave María purísima,*" Abuela said, taking the scissors out of my hand. "What did that box ever do to you to deserve an attack like that?"

"I just want to see what's inside," I said.

"*Paciencia, hija,*" Abuela said. She took the scissors and carefully opened the box.

Inside was a letter for Abuela and a letter for me. Mami had sent Abuela a pair of comfy slippers, pink with little satin ribbons on them.

"Nice," Abuela said, trying them on.

There were also two miniskirts with matching tops.

I opened Mami's letter where she explained that the two outfits were for me and "*nuestra vecina*, the girl next door, Ana."

I went over to Ana's right away and knocked hard on the door.

"Hey, Ana," I called into the open window of her apartment. "*Apúrate.*"

Ana opened the door of her apartment. "Yo, Marisol, what's up?"

I smiled as I walked into Ana's apartment. It made me laugh the way Ana was always trying to talk like me, using American words like yo.

"Ana, my *mami* sent a surprise for you," I said, taking the outfits from behind my back.

Each outfit had a denim miniskirt. One top was green, the other bright orange.

"This is so nice. I've never even met your mother," Ana said, a big smile coming to her face.

"But I told her all about you," I explained.

"Which one is mine?" Ana said, her eyes moving from the orange top to the green one.

"It's up to you," I said.

"*Naranja,*" Ana said, picking up the orange T-shirt and one of the skirts.

"*Por supuesto,*" I said, smiling. "I know how you like your clothes to be bright."

I could hardly sleep the night before Ana and I had planned to go down to the Wilcox Building. After lying awake for a long time, I decided to get up and write a letter to Magda.

Dear Magda,

Hopefully, by the time you get this letter, I will have found my father. Tomorrow, Ana and I are going to the building where he once lived when he first met Mami. We don't think he'll be there, but it will be a good place to start looking for clues.

I'm sorry that your summer was so rotten, Magda. Panama is better than I thought it would be, but tienes que recordar, I started school the first week of August. I had almost no summer vacation. I like school, but not that much. Next summer will be better, for both of us. Te prometo.

I almost had a heart attack when I read in your letter that Evelyn was helping you out with your drill team routine. Qué milagro lo de Evelyn. I would wish you good luck on the tryouts, but I know you don't need it.

I stopped writing for a second, chewing the pen cap as I tried to figure out what else to say. I touched my necklace, my *pequeña cruz.* Then I continued writing.

Pray for me, Magda. Pray that I'll find my papi soon.

Con cariño, tu mejor amiga,
Marisol

The next day I was up and dressed before Ana started pounding on Abuela's door.

"You're both up so early," Abuela said as she let Ana in.

"We're going down to——" Ana started to say.

"——*the park*," I said, finishing Ana's sentence.

"It's a perfectly good Saturday," I continued. "Why waste a whole day sleeping?"

"Hmm," Abuela said, returning to her *café* and newspaper. "A perfectly good Saturday never stopped you from sleeping late before."

Abuela looked both me and Ana up and down, then walked in a circle, looking at our clothes, our hair, and our knapsacks.

"Okay, you can go," Abuela finally said. *"Ten cuidado."*

"Are you sure you know which bus it is?" I asked as we walked down to the bus stop.

"Of course," Ana said calmly.

"Do you think he'll be there?" I asked.

"I don't know," Ana said. "It's been such a long time

since he lived there. But I hope we find him, for your sake."

We walked in silence for a moment, then Ana turned to me.

"Marisol?"

"Yeah," I answered.

"Do you like chicken?" she asked.

"What?" I answered. This was hardly the time to talk about food.

"Do you like chicken?" she asked again, smiling.

"Yeah, but—"

"Then grab a wing," Ana said, hooking her elbow around mine.

"Oh, Ana, you're just so *cheesy*," I said.

"Cheesy?" she repeated, wrinkling her nose. "That doesn't sound so good."

"It means silly," I explained as we walked up to the bus stop.

"Chee-sy," Ana said again, dragging out the *e*.

"The *cheesiest*," I said, laughing.

14

We got off the bus at Ninth Street. "Do you remember which one is the Wilcox Building?" I asked, my stomach turning.

"It's the tall yellow building at the top of that street," Ana said, pointing ahead of us.

We walked toward the Wilcox and the closer we got, the more I wanted to climb back on the bus and go back home to Abuela's. What if Papi didn't want to see me? What if he was mean and fat and bald? A million *What if's* pulsated through my brain.

When we got to the building, I knocked on one of the first-floor doors and said, "*Estoy buscando a* Lucho Mayaguez."

The woman who answered the door was short, with fake-blond hair and greasy skin. A cigarette dangled from the side of her mouth. I was surprised it didn't fall out while she spoke.

"You're a lot younger than the other girls who are always asking about him," the woman said, letting out a little laugh.

Ana didn't seem frightened by her at all, but I was.

"What room is it?" Ana asked.

The woman glared at her. "Apartment 2B," she said.

Slowly I followed Ana up the stairs.

"Be here, Lucho," I prayed silently. "Be here and fill the hole in my heart."

At the top of the staircase, I stared at the door to apartment 2B. I smoothed back my twists, then doublechecked the straps of my sundress.

"Do I look all right?" I asked.

"You look terrific," Ana said, squeezing my hand.

I made the sign of the cross quickly, then touched the little cross around my neck.

"Wish me luck, Magda," I whispered as I walked toward the door.

I knocked softly, my hands trembling the whole time.

"There's no answer," I whispered to Ana. "Let's go."

Upstairs, a dog started to bark wildly, but no one in apartments 2A or 2B seemed to stir.

"No one could hear a knock like that," Ana said, banging loudly on the door.

I heard the sound of heavy feet coming toward the door and I jumped back.

"Who is it?" a man's voice called. Then a man came to the door. I just stared at him, unable to say anything. He was wearing the same kind of white T-shirt as the guy in my picture. But he was older, in his thirties, like Mami. If this was Lucho, he had gained a lot of weight, but I thought I could see some similarities in the face. I thought about the picture in my knapsack and wondered if I should take it out.

"*Qué quieres, niña?*" the man asked me. Ana stood at the railing of the building, looking down onto the street.

"*Nosotttttraaass* . . . we . . . ," I stammered, pointing to Ana and myself, all the Spanish I had learned over the last three months escaping me.

I took a deep breath and began again. "*Es usted* Lucho Mayaguez?"

The man laughed a big belly laugh as if I had just said the funniest thing he had ever heard.

"*Ay caramba, no,*" he said. "I'm his brother, Oscar."

My heart had been beating so fast when I climbed the stairs, now I could feel it sinking into my stomach like a balloon that was losing air.

"Is Lucho here?" I asked, trying to look around the big man in front of me.

"Who are you, little girl?" Oscar Mayaguez asked.

"I'm his daughter," I told him. "I guess that would make me *su sobrina*, your niece."

Oscar stepped back and rubbed his eyes as if to wake himself up.

"Wait a second," he said. "You're Inez's little baby girl?"

"Yes," I said. "I'm Inez's daughter."

"Don't you live in *Nueva York*?" Oscar asked.

I nodded, trying to fight back my tears. I didn't want to be talking to him, I wanted to find my father. I needed to know where he was.

"You came all this way to find Lucho?" Oscar asked.

I nodded again, but I gave up on trying to hold in my tears. They escaped my eyes, one at a time, rolling down my cheeks.

"I wish I could help you," Oscar said, offering me his handkerchief. "Lucho's been gone for years now. I took over his room. He works in the country now. I hear from him every once in a while, but he doesn't have a phone number or a steady address. He could be anywhere."

Ana stood beside me and put her arm around my shoulder.

"Thank you, *señor*," she said as I cried softly. "Come on, Marisol. It's time to go home."

I tried to give my uncle back his wet handkerchief, but he shook his head no. "You keep it," he said. Then he spoke to Ana.

"*Cuídala*," he said. "You take care of her."

On the bus I sat next to Ana, staring down at the embroidered handkerchief in my hand. I hadn't noticed before the carefully stitched navy blue letters in the right-hand corner. LM.

I held the handkerchief out to Ana.

"Look at this," I said. "When I started crying, Oscar gave me his handkerchief. But the monogram says LM—Lucho Mayaguez. This must belong to my father."

Ana nodded.

I folded the handkerchief carefully and put it in my knapsack.

Ana and I got off the bus near Abuela's apartment and walked down to the park.

"Do you think we could go to the country and see if we could find him?" I asked Ana.

Ana shook her head. "*El campo*, the country, is just an expression," she explained. "It's like when Americans say 'the south.' It could mean anywhere."

"What am I going to do?" I asked. I was curled up like a ball on the bench, my knees tucked in front of me.

"I don't think there's much you *can* do," Ana said. "*Ya veras*. You're going to be here until the spring. Maybe he'll come find you."

I thought about how many times I had dreamed about my father coming to New York to look for me. In my head, I had imagined all the sweet conversations we might have; how loving and close we would be. Now I was in Panama and I wasn't any closer to finding Lucho Mayaguez than I had been in New York.

That night I took my father's picture and his handkerchief and laid them side by side on my dresser. Then for the first time in a long time, I knelt down and prayed.

Dear God, I prayed silently. Prove that Mami was wrong and that I was right. Please let my father come looking for me. Please reunite us, I want to know my father so badly, God. Amen.

I got up, and before I turned out the lights in my room, I pressed the photograph of Lucho to my chest.

"Don't let me down, Papi," I whispered.

Then I went to bed.

15

I was running down the hallway to meet Ana for lunch when Mrs. Ortiz grabbed my shoulder.

"*Buenos días*, Señora Ortiz," I said proudly, finally getting the hang of greeting everyone in Spanish. I knew I still sounded American, but it didn't bother me as much anymore.

"Marisol, I would like to invite you to perform for *un baile típico* for the Christmas dance celebration," Mrs. Ortiz said. The minute I heard the word *dance*, I started to turn and walk away.

Mrs. Ortiz put her hand on my shoulder and turned me back around. "*Qué pasa*, Marisol?" she asked. "You don't like to dance?"

"I'm a terrible dancer, Mrs. Ortiz," I said.

"*No hay tal cosa*, I'm choreographing the dances," she said. "I'll be happy to give you as much help as you need.

"We'll be doing the *baile típico*, the national dance, as well as other traditional Latin American dances," Mrs. Ortiz explained. "I think it will be a great experience for your year abroad. We'll meet tomorrow after school in the gym."

Then Mrs. Ortiz gave my shoulder a little tap and walked away.

I found Ana on the lunch line.

"*Hola*, Marisol," she said. "What's going on?"

I stuck out my tongue as if I'd just had some bad medicine. "It sucks to be me."

Ana gave me a curious look. "It *sucks* to be you?"

Secretly, I loved the way that Ana repeated everything I said. She thought all of my New York expressions like "fly" and "dope" were the ultimate in cool. Whenever I said a New York expression that Ana had never heard, she'd be repeating it even when the expression didn't make any sense to her.

"Mrs. Ortiz wants me to do the *baile típico* in the Christmas dance celebration," I explained.

"*Qué chévere,*" Ana said. "Very cool. I always dance in the celebration. Rubén does, too. It's a lot of fun."

"Fun for *you*, maybe," I said, groaning and picking at the slimy stuff on my plate that was supposed to be *arroz con pollo*, chicken with rice. I wondered if there was some sort of international law that wherever you went in the world, school cafeteria food *had* to be disgusting.

"I'll help you learn the baile típico, Marisol," Ana said, smiling. "It will be *dope*."

"Dope?" I laughed. "I doubt it. But I'll give it a shot."

One thing I had learned about being the foreign student was that everyone was always offering to help me out. They really wanted me to feel as comfortable as I would at home.

Little did they know that at home, I was hardly Miss Popularity. It was strange, but in some ways, I was more comfortable in Panama than in New York. Something was happening in Panama. I was still Marisol, but a *better* Marisol; a stronger, smarter Marisol who spoke Spanish and could travel in two different worlds. I always thought Panama was only about Mami and the *tías*, about faded photographs in an old leather album.

Looking at Ana across the cafeteria table, I knew that I'd never forget her orange-tinted glasses, the way the sun bounced off the water at the beach, the palm trees, and Abuela's sweet smell. Coming to Panama had taught me that only pictures fade. Memories always stay alive in living color.

Of course, Abuela thought my joining Mrs. Ortiz's dance group was a wonderful idea.

"I'll make you a *pollera*, the traditional outfit for

dancing the *baile típico*," she said. "We'll go shopping for fabric on Saturday."

"No, Abuela, you should wait," I said. "I don't want you to waste your money. I'm not a very good dancer. At home, Roxana always laughs when I try to dance salsa."

"Sit down, *niña*," Abuela said.

At Abuela's, we always had a snack late in the evening before going to bed, and I had begun to look forward to this time every evening when we could talk. Abuela put a pot of hot tea on the table and cut me a piece of fruity bun.

"What is this obsession you have with your cousin, Roxana?" she asked.

"I don't know," I said quietly, picking raisins out of the bun.

"You do know," Abuela insisted.

"Roxana hates me," I said.

"Your cousin doesn't hate you," Abuela said.

My face grew hot. Abuela didn't understand. She was just like Mami. She'd forgotten what it was like to be thirteen and how mean girls like Roxana could be. Abuela was a grandmother. To her, it probably seemed like it had been a hundred years since someone had picked on her.

"When you were just a baby, my oldest daughter, your Tía Julia went to America," Abuela began, sweetening her tea with honey.

"Julia took her two youngest children, Manuel and Paula, with her. But Roxana was the oldest child. She was afraid to leave Panama. She didn't want to leave her friends and her school."

I shook my head in disbelief. "I can't imagine Roxana afraid of anything."

"That's because you're picturing her as a proud six-teen-year-old girl with a saucy mouth," Abuela said, laughing a little. "Try to picture Roxana as an eight-year-old, a girl much younger than you."

I thought for a second and remembered a picture Mami had in her album. It was a picture of Roxana in front of Ruinas de Panama la Vieja, the oldest part of Panama City. The Ruinas was an old tower that had survived the great fire when Panama was burned down in the 1500s. I'd heard Mami talk about the Ruinas ever since I was a little kid.

"I told Julia to take the babies," Abuela continued her story. "Roxana stayed with me. She stayed for five years. She didn't want to go to New York, you know? She cried and screamed for weeks. She was so happy here in Panama. But she needed to be with her mother, she needed the education she could only get in the States."

Abuela put her hand on her chest and sighed deeply. "Roxana was *mi corazón*, my heart," she said.

"But at home, Roxana is so mean to me," I tried to

explain. I couldn't believe how Abuela talked about Roxana as if she were this kind, sweet person. Besides, I was the one living in Panama now. I was supposed to be Abuela's *corazón*.

"Very few people are mean all the time to everyone," Abuela said, as if I should understand this by now. "You've only seen one part of Roxana, and it's not the best part. There's more to her, I promise. I think if you tried to get to know her, you could be more than cousins. You could be friends."

"*As if*," I muttered.

"What did you say?" Abuela asked.

"*I wish*," I said, giving Abuela my sweetest smile.

No way could Roxana and I be friends. She was La Evil herself. Abuela couldn't see it because she was a grandmother. She had to love all of her grandchildren.

But I knew better.

"I still don't want to do this dance thing, Abuelita," I said, using the loving term of her name, Abuelita, instead of Abuela.

"Try it tomorrow and then we'll talk in the evening," Abuela suggested. "I always dreamed that I would be able to make a beautiful *pollera* for my American grand-daughter. Every year at Christmas, I go to the school and see the children dance. It would make me so proud to see you dancing with them."

I made a face. "No pressure, right?"

She smiled and crossed her heart. "No pressure at all, preciosa."

That night, I wrote Magda a letter.

Querida Magda,

What's up, girl? I'm doing pretty well. Have you gotten my letters? Qué paso? *You can't say that you didn't understand them, because I always write to you in Spanglish. I know how much you love to mix your Spanish with English. If they taught Spanglish instead of Spanish in school, you'd be an A student. (smile) I know you must have been busy, starting the eighth grade and everything. But I can't believe I've only gotten two letters from you, and* nada *since school started!* Tu mejor amiga, y me has abandonado. *I've already written you close to* fifteen *letters. I write you* cada semana *and you play me like a trick deck of cards.*

I can't believe that I've been down here for five months. Think about it, Magda. I'm almost halfway done. In seven more months, I'll be back home. Cómo te fue en los tryouts del drill team? *I know you made the team because you're the best dancer in the eighth grade. When I come back, you've got to teach me all the steps, so I can make the team, too. You know I'm not exactly the most coordinated person.*

Which leads me to the real news of this letter—
Abuela and my guidance counselor, Mrs. Ortiz, are making
me dance in a performance. You know that I'm shy, no
quiero hacerlo. If it was just a school dance, I could try
and do some of the fly moves that you taught me and it
wouldn't be so bad. But it's Latin dancing and we're
going to be on stage, and I'm sure that I'm going to make
a fool of myself.

I NEED YOUR ADVICE! Write me as soon as you get
this letter because the mail takes forever to get down here.

I can hardly believe that it's only three weeks until
Christmas. It's very strange. There are Christmas decora-
tions everywhere, but it's eighty-five degrees out and we're
all still wearing shorts. Is it snowing in New York? Send
me a picture. I wish I was there to team up with you for
those snowball fights!

Miss me because I miss you.

Your best friend,
(even though you've been dissing me)
Marisol

P. S. Abuela spent the better part of the evening trying
to convince me that Roxana was actually a sweet, kind
human being and not the demon child we know her to be.
Yeah, right. De boba, no tengo nada.

16

All day in class, I kept wondering how I could get out of dancing the *baile típico*. I thought about cutting out of school, sneaking home to Abuela's, and dealing with the consequences later. But when I got out of my last class, Mrs. Ortiz was standing at the door waiting for me.

"*Buenos días*, Marisol," she said, smiling. "I checked your schedule and thought it might be nice if I met you here. We can walk over to the gym together."

"You'll be sorry," I muttered as Mrs. Ortiz and I walked down the hall.

"No, *you'll* be the one who will be sorry if you don't give the *baile* a chance, *niña*," Mrs. Ortiz said. "This isn't some sort of dance contest. It's about enjoying ourselves and preserving our heritage. You'll see," she promised.

Inside the gym there was a circle of kids. I knew Rubén and Ana and some of the other eighth graders, but about half of them were ninth graders who I didn't know at all. I was the only American in the whole place.

"You'll have to choose partners," Mrs. Ortiz told the group, and unlike the kids in my old school, nobody groaned or made stupid faces.

Rubén walked right up to me. "Will you be my partner?" he asked.

I shook my head, and whispered, "*Escúchame*, Rubén. Listen to me. I'm a terrible dancer."

Rubén took my hand and I tried to keep it from trembling. What made it worse was that Rubén didn't let me go. He just gave my hand a little squeeze and said, "*No hay problema.*"

Once everyone had picked partners, the girls lined up on one side of the room and the boys on the other. Mrs. Ortiz went over to the old-fashioned record player (nobody in Panama seemed to have CD players) and started to play a traditional *ritmo*.

The room was filled with the sound of congas and drums, guitars that were strumming so quickly, the rhythms popped like hot oil in a frying pan. I smiled as I recognized the music. "Farolito" was an old Christmas song that my mother liked to sing. My mother always sang it to me as a bedtime lullaby. This version was faster, the music that surrounded it was fuller. But the words were the same:

Farolito sea en el cielo
Poco a poco va naciendo
Como nace el sentimiento
En las calles de mi pueblo
Como nace el sentimiento
En las calles de mi pueblo.

Corazón que canta
Corazón que sueña
Lleno de esperanza
En la noche buena.

Mami had first translated the words of the song for me when I was a little girl. A *farolito* was a little star, and the song was all about the hope and joy of Christmas Eve. In Spanish, Christmas Eve was known as *la noche buena* or "the good night," because Jesus is about to be born. Although I still struggled with my Spanish, I knew the song so well that I could translate all the words:

Little star that shines in the sky
Bit by bit, you are being born
As the feeling is being born
in the streets of my village
As the feeling is being born
in the streets of my village.

The heart that sings
The heart that dreams
So full of hope
for the holy night.

As I sang along to the words, I thought about New York and all the feelings that had been born on the streets there. Brooklyn was like my village, and this was going to be my first Christmas away from home. The song reminded me so much of Mami, and I wished she could be here to share *la navidad verde* with me and Abuela. Mami had always said that in Panama, you had a "green Christmas" because there was nothing but palm trees everywhere. Even in December.

I turned and caught Rubén giving me a funny look. Then I realized why. While I had been singing aloud, everyone else was watching Mrs. Ortiz go through the movements.

"You know the words, eh?" Rubén teased as he danced a little two-step around me.

I nodded. "My mother's been singing me this song ever since I was a little girl."

"Maybe you're more Panamanian than you think, Mar-i-sol," Rubén said, dragging my name out.

Mrs. Ortiz walked down the row of boys and girls, stopping by each student and helping them with the movements of the *baile*. It seemed simple enough—two steps forward, two steps back—but we all had to do it in unison and our feet had to stamp out the rhythm of the conga.

"First the feet," Mrs. Ortiz said. "Don't be afraid to stomp your feet hard, *fuerte ahora*."

We tried to follow Mrs. Ortiz, but everyone was stepping to a different rhythm. We sounded like a herd of elephants, not a group of dancers.

"*Alto, alto*," Mrs. Ortiz said, putting her hands over her ears and cringing. "I've got another idea.

"I want everybody to jump up and down like me," Mrs. Ortiz said, and she started to bounce up and down as if she was on a trampoline.

Everyone followed her, jumping up and down. Rubén did these fancy jumps, kicking midair, as if he was on his skateboard. Ana and I kept looking at each other and laughing.

"Jump as if you were jumping for joy," Mrs. Ortiz called out. "*Estén felices, muy felices*. Happy to be jumping.

"Okay, *ya*," Mrs. Ortiz said. "Enough jumping. When you do the step, put that kind of happiness into it. Every time your feet hit the ground, stomp down as if you were having the happiest time of your life."

Mrs. Ortiz walked over to the record player and

started the music again. "Now, start," she said. "Two steps forward. Two steps back."

We all stomped back and forth, as if we'd never been happier. But nobody was dancing in time with their partners, much less anybody else.

Mrs. Ortiz walked over to the record player and turned it off again.

"I have *another* idea," she said, holding her hands up, urging us to stop.

We all looked at each other and giggled.

"We'll start the *paseo*, two dancers at a time," she said.

"First, Clara and Roberto," she said. "Try it without the music. "

Clara and Roberto were ninth graders, and they started doing the steps in perfect rhythm.

"Very good, keep going," Mrs. Ortiz said, walking down the line. "Now, I want Angelica and Jaime to follow them."

Angelica and Jaime stood next to Clara and Roberto and stepped right into their rhythm.

Mrs. Ortiz applauded. "*Magnífico*! Don't stop dancing. Now Ana and Raul."

Ana was dancing with an eighth grader named Raul. He was in my science class, and by the way he kept biting his bottom lip, I could tell he was even more nervous about dancing than I was.

"Don't worry, Raul," Mrs. Ortiz said, putting her arm around him. "Follow me."

Mrs. Ortiz danced next to Raul until he got into the rhythm, too.

By the time Mrs. Ortiz called out, "Rubén y Marisol!" I wasn't scared anymore. I stomped forward and backward, then forward again. Rubén smiled and gave me a thumbs-up.

"*Muy bien,*" he said, "Very good. We'll make a *salsera* out of you yet."

"*Veremos,*" I answered. "We'll see."

"Now the hands," Mrs. Ortiz called. "For the young men, it's easy; the hands are either behind your back or bent in front of you, as if you're holding a huge bowl of fruit.

"Young ladies, I want you to practice twirling your wrists, one time, two times, then clapping, fast and quick."

As Mrs. Ortiz danced I was struck by how beautiful she was, the way her dark skin glistened with a thin layer of sweat, and the way her long, thick braid bounced against her back. She was tall, with a curvy figure, and when she did the hand movements, every muscle in her body seemed to roll like drops of water pouring down the outside of a pitcher.

Soon we were all clapping and stomping to the rhythm of the music.

"*Corazón que canta,*" the song went. And we answered with our bodies: stomp, stomp, clap, clap.

"*Corazón que sueña.*"

Stomp, stomp. Clap, clap.

We were just getting the hang of it when Mrs. Ortiz said that we were finished for the day.

"Next Tuesday," she said, laughing at our disappointed sighs. "And every Tuesday until Christmas!"

The two neat rows of boys and girls scattered. Ana introduced me to some eighth-grade girls I didn't know, while Rubén and his friends started shooting hoops with somebody's ball.

"Marisol, can I see you for a second?" Mrs. Ortiz asked. She was locking the records and record player into the storage closet.

A chill raced through me when she called my name. I'd had so much fun learning the dance. The hand that Rubén held still tingled with a strange kind of electricity. I couldn't wait for the next rehearsal. I loved learning the *baile típico* and being Rubén's partner.

Mrs. Ortiz is going to tell me that I wasn't good enough to stay in the group, I thought.

"Yes, Mrs. Ortiz" I said, standing stiff as a board.

"About our conversation yesterday, Marisol—" Mrs. Ortiz began in a serious voice.

"I know what you're going to say," I said, trying to interrupt her.

"I can choose only sixteen students to dance in the performance and—"

"I know, I know," I said, turning my face away, so she wouldn't see how pitiful I looked.

"That's why I'm very happy that I asked you to join us," Mrs. Ortiz said, smiling.

"So I can stay?" I asked.

"Of course you can stay," Mrs. Ortiz said. "See you next Tuesday."

By the time we'd finish talking, all the students had left. Ana was waiting for me at the gym door.

"Rubén had to leave, but he asked me to give you this," she said, handing me a note.

I looked at the note for a second, wondering what Rubén could have written to me. Then I quickly slipped it into my skirt pocket.

"Aren't you going to read it?" Ana asked.

"I'll read it later," I said, trying to be as cool as Magda would be.

But Ana wasn't having it. "I saw him holding your hand," she said. "He's so cute and now he's going to be your *novio*, your boyfriend."

"Not necessarily," I said. But the way I was being so cool sounded unconvincing, even to me.

We walked out of the school building and headed home.

"You're lucky," Ana said after a few minutes. "I've never had a boyfriend before."

I thought about how I'd felt back in New York, when I saw Magda flirting with Stephen Cardoza. I thought Magda was so cool and that I'd never be that comfortable around a guy. But now I was as cool as Magda.

I didn't say anything, I just gave Ana a tight hug.

"I never had a boyfriend in New York," I admitted.

"Marisol—" Ana said, pausing for a second.

"Uh-huh," I answered.

"Do you still think it 'sucks to be you'?"

"Okay, you win," I said, giving her a fake punch on the arm. "Let's read Rubén's note."

We sat down on the steps of the library. I could feel my hands shake a little as I pulled the letter out of my pocket. It said:

Dear Marisol, you are the prettiest girl in our school and not just because you're from New York and really cool. You're beautiful on the inside, too. I'm honored to be your friend. Will you do me the even greater honor of being my girlfriend?

Sincerely,
Rubén Romero

I looked over at Ana, grabbed her hand, and the two of us screamed.

"I can't believe it!" I said. "But you know Abuela would kill me if she knew I had a boyfriend."

"She doesn't have to know," Ana said, giggling. "Rubén is such a nice guy. And this letter, it's, how would you say it, pretty dope, no?"

"*Ultra-dope*, Ana," I said, folding the letter up and putting it back in my pocket.

"So what do I say?" I asked as we stood up and continued walking home.

"Say yes," Ana said. *"Di que sí."*

When we arrived at our building, Ana went home. But I stood outside on the porch by myself, wondering if it wasn't all a dream. I looked down Parque LeFevre Street, the palm trees high above me, the smell of the ocean, fried fish, and sugarcane all around me.

It had been two months since we'd gone to the Wilcox Building, looking for Lucho. I don't want to say I gave up on my dream of meeting him. But little by little, I'd stopped wishing every day for him to show up. It was so much easier to love people I could see and touch, like Abuela and Ana. It was easier to love people like Mami and Magda who I know loved me back.

Lucho was just a picture. I didn't know his voice, his

smell, the feel of my cheek against his. And sometimes trying to love him felt like trying to put my arms around a pocket of air. Empty.

Ana was right. I was so lucky, not just to have met Rubén, but to have a friend like her. No, it didn't suck to be me. Not at all.

17

I was practicing English with Rubén in the library when he asked me if I wanted a surfing lesson.

"No way," I said, shaking my head.

"Oh, come on," Rubén said, grinning. *"Por lo menos, piensalo."*

Over the past few weeks, we had settled into a steady routine. We met during second period to practice our English and Spanish. Then we met up in the playground during lunch. I'd never met up with Rubén outside of school, but we held hands in the hallway and slipped each other notes every day.

"Well, let's go to the beach on Saturday," Rubén said.

"I don't know," I answered. *"Mi abuela es muy estricta.* She thought letting my *mami* date at the age of sixteen was a big deal."

"No te preocupes," Rubén said, his dreads hanging in

front of his eyes. "I'll come by your house and talk to your *abuela*."

"*Te voy a dar un consejo*," I said, closing my notebook right before the bell rang. "Don't stand on the street and holler for me to come downstairs. She hates that. The last guy that did that got a bucket of dirty water on his head."

"Whoo, *tu abuela es un poco tiesa, eh?*" Rubén said, following me out of the library. "That's kind of rough."

That night, when Abuela and I had our evening snack before bed, I sipped on my tea and wondered how to bring Rubén up.

"Abuela," I said, "There's something I want to talk to you about."

"That's funny," she said, smiling. "There's something I want to talk to you about, as well. You first."

I walked over to her and gave her a big kiss. "*Abuelita, Abuela de mi alma.*"

"What is it?" Abuela said. "*Qué quieres, niña?*"

"Well, you know my friend Rubén, from school?" I asked.

"The boy who calls here so much you would think his mother works for the telephone company?" Abuela asked, twisting her mouth to one side.

"He's only called me like five times," I said. "Abuela, *no dígas cuentos.*"

"What about him?" she said.

"He invited me to go to the beach," I said. "He wants to come here on Saturday and talk to you."

"Ya vamos de nuevo," Abuela said. "He can come, but if I don't like the looks of him, you're not going anywhere."

"Don't worry," I said, beaming. "You'll like him."

"Veremos," Abuela said. "We'll see."

"So what is your news?" I asked.

"We'll be having some visitors for Christmas," Abuela began.

"Mami!" I yelled, jumping out of my seat. Christmas was only three weeks away; the dance concert was in two weeks. But just last week, Mami had said she wasn't coming because the tickets were too expensive.

"She called today while you were at school," Abuela explained. "She got some sort of great bargain airfare. She'll be here in two weeks. But she's not the only one who's coming."

"Tía China?" I asked.

Abuela shook her head no.

"Tía Julia?" I asked.

"Nope," Abuela said, smiling.

"Not Roxana," I groaned.

"Marisol," Abuela said in a serious voice. "That's your cousin, your blood."

"Okay, sorry," I said.

"It's not Roxana," Abuela said, raising her eyebrows.

"Magda?" I asked, hopefully.

Abuela nodded and said, "So now I will get a chance to meet the infamous Magdalena Rosario."

"Yes," I said, throwing my arms up in the air. "When do they get here?"

"They're coming in two weeks to see you dance the *baile típico*," Abuela said. "Speaking of which, come try on your dress."

I followed Abuela into the living room. She had been working on my *pollera*, the traditional Panamanian formal dress, for weeks. She wouldn't let me see it. She said it was a surprise.

"But what if I want you to change something?"

"What is there to change?" she said, throwing her hands up in a shrug. "It's a *traditional* dress. You just can't change it to suit your style."

Now, Abuela opened a large paper shopping bag and lifted out an armful of lace and satin.

She held it up in front of herself and asked, "So what do you think?"

"*Bellísimo,*" I said, trying not to cry. "It's the most beautiful dress I've ever seen."

The dress was white with hundreds of layers of lace and emerald-green satin stitched in every row. It was kind of sexy too, pulling down onto the shoulders so that the neckline would be completely bare.

I tried on the dress, and as I lifted it up over my head, I saw that the inside was completely lined with emerald satin. Even where no one was going to see it, Abuela had taken the time to make sure that the dress was fabulous, inside and out. When she said, *"Las cosas se hacen bien o no se hacen*. Do things right or not at all," she really meant it.

I stood still as Abuela zipped the back of the dress. Then lifting the dress a little so it wouldn't drag on the floor, I walked slowly to the bathroom.

The girl staring at me from the full-length mirror looked like a dream. A head full of jet-black twists, deep chocolate-brown skin, and a fairy-tale dress that looked like something Cinderella's fairy godmother might have whipped up.

I remembered the conversation I'd had so many months before with Magda at her house. It was before I knew that I was coming to Panama, and I still dreamed that Junior Vasquez would be my date for my *quinceañera*. I looked in the mirror and thought, "Junior Vasquez, *mira lo que te perdiste*. Look at me now."

Abuela stood beside me, looking at me in the mirror.

"It's not so bad," she said, tilting her head sideways and fiddling with a piece of lace on the dress.

"It's *perfect*," I said, hugging her and holding her close. "Thank you, Abuelita. Thank you for everything."

That Saturday, Rubén came over to talk to Abuela. It was a little after noon when he arrived, but I had been up for hours. When I heard the knock on the door, I opened it, and there he was.

Rubén had pulled his dreadlocks back with a rubber band and he was wearing ironed clothes: a white shirt, and tan linen shorts. I looked down and smiled when I saw that he was wearing leather sandals and not his usual sneakers.

"*Qué guapo*. You look good," I said approvingly.

"So do you," he answered.

Abuela stood behind me and cleared her throat.

"Rubén," I said, turning to Abuela. "This is my grandmother, Mrs. Velásquez."

"*Mucho gusto en conocerla*," Rubén said, shaking her hand. "It's a pleasure to meet you."

"Have a seat," Abuela said, gesturing for Rubén to sit on the couch. I sat next to him. Abuela sat in her favorite armchair.

"You have a beautiful home," Rubén said, looking around.

"Gracias," Abuela said.

I had to smile at the first-class treatment she was giving Rubén. She had even changed from her housedress into the same flower-print dress she had worn to pick me up at the airport.

Abuela got up and walked into the kitchen.

"Rubén," she called out. "Are you hungry?"

"Say yes," I whispered to him.

Abuela had been up since seven o'clock making all kinds of *frituras*, including my favorite *empanadas*. She would have been really offended if Rubén didn't eat anything.

"I'm starving," Rubén said, winking at me. "I wanted to make sure and be on time, so I didn't get a chance to eat breakfast."

Abuela came back with a platter full of *frituras*. She shook her finger at Rubén. "You should always eat breakfast," she said. "If you have to be someplace, get up earlier."

Rubén just smiled and helped himself to a *tamale*.

"So what are your plans for this afternoon?" Abuela asked.

Rubén looked nervous for a second and shifted in his seat.

"I would like to take Marisol for a walk on the beach," Rubén said. "Then for some ice cream downtown. We would be home by six o'clock."

"That sounds fine," Abuela said.

It was all I could do not to jump for joy. But I knew it wouldn't do to act too excited.

"Thank you, Abuela," I said, giving her a kiss.

Rubén and I finished eating every *fritura* Abuela had put out. I reached down for another *empanada* and saw that there were just crumbs. We both looked down at the empty plate and laughed.

"You must have been hungry," Abuela said. "You better head out if you're really planning on being back by six.

"I hope to see you again, Rubén," Abuela said, giving him a hug. "You should come over for dinner sometime before Christmas. You can meet Marisol's mother, who will be visiting from New York."

Rubén looked over at me and said, "Hey, your *mami* is coming from New York. That's great."

"I know," I said, fastening my orange knapsack. "My best friend, Magda, is coming too."

"*Cuídate.* Be careful out there," Abuela said, kissing me on the cheek. "Call if you're going to be late."

Rubén and I sat at the edge of the beach all afternoon. We had taken off our shoes; it felt good to have the waves wash over my feet and to press my toes into the sand.

"I had so much fun today," Rubén said, turning to me. "I've never met anyone like you."

Then he leaned over and kissed me, very lightly, on the lips. The kiss wasn't anything like I'd imagined.

Back home there had been a television show that Magda and I loved to watch. Whenever a guy was about to kiss someone on that show, the actor always yelled out, "I'm coming in," before he planted a wet one on the girl's face.

Magda and I used to joke about it all the time.

"I'm coming in," we'd say in deep voices, laughing hysterically as we grabbed a pillow and kissed it.

I couldn't wait to tell Magda that guys didn't always say that before they kissed a girl. I thought about her and Stephen Cardoza and wondered if she already knew.

"*Mar y sol,*" Rubén said. "You are the sea and the sun."

"What are you talking about?" I said.

"Don't you know?" Rubén said. "Your name, it comes from the Spanish words for sea and sun. *Mar y sol.*"

"I never knew that," I said, smiling. "'That's really cool."

I remembered then what Abuela had said about Panama meaning "abundance of fishes."

"Everything has a meaning," Abuela had said. "Even if you don't know what it is."

I looked out at the ocean, then gazed up at the sun.

It had taken my coming to Panama to learn the meaning of so many things: my family, my heritage, my language, even my name.

My father was still a mystery, but that didn't make me sad the way it used to. I had filled the hole in my heart with new loves, like Ana, Rubén, and Abuela. Like Mami, I was learning to love on two continents, learning to love in two languages. Like Mami, there was room in my heart for a whole lot of people.

If and when my father ever showed up, there would be room for him, too.

Quinceañera means ♥ sweet 15

NEW! coming soon

sneak preview chapter

1

No money, no *quince*, no dress. I tried to explain this to my best friend, Magdalena Rosario, as we headed toward the bus stop. But the girl had a mind of her own. *"No seas tan negativa,"* Magda said, wagging a finger at me. "We'll figure this out."

"This" being the question of my "Sweet 15" party, or *quinceañera*. The fact was that my mom didn't have the money to throw me a big bash and Magda's family had been saving for her *quince* practically since the day she was born. Magda's sister, Evelyn, had had a huge *quince* the year before. Now it was Magda's turn, and she could hardly wait. Which was why, for the third time in a week, we were on our way to the mall to look at *quince* dresses.

"I don't know why you won't just have a double *quince* with me," Magda said, reaching into her pocket for a MetroCard to pay the busfare.

It was a cool November afternoon in Brooklyn, where we live. I could see the bus ambling toward us and felt a cold wind on my face. It hadn't snowed yet, but it would soon.

"Hello?" Magda said, shaking a head full of wavy jet-black hair in my face. "Am I talking to myself?"

I smiled. "I'm sorry, Magda," I said. "I was thinking about snow."

Magda grimaced as she pulled her puffy pink jacket tighter around her neck.

"Don't even say that word to me!" Magda said. "I bet you didn't miss the snow when you were in Panama."

"Qué piensas?" I laughed. "You know I didn't."

A little over a year before, when I was thirteen, I had gone to live with my *abuela*, my grandmother, in Panama, while my mom finished graduate school. At first, I thought I was going to hate it. I'd never met my grandmother before. I'd never even visited Panama. I was born here, in the U.S. of A. I was so afraid of leaving Mami and my best friend, Magda. When Mami first brought up the idea she didn't understand why I was so upset.

"You're going *home*," she would say excitedly.

"*Your* home," I muttered for weeks. "You're the one from Panama, not me."

But though I hated to admit it, Mami *tenía razón*. If Panama didn't feel like home at first, that quickly changed. I fell in love with Abuela and I made some great friends.

Going away, though, made things pretty funky between me and Magda. Even though I'd been back for almost six months, she still brought up my going to Panama all the time, as if she was afraid that I was going to up and leave her at any given moment.

I'd be lying if I said that Panama hadn't changed me. Before I went away, I pretty much depended on Magda for everything. Her mom and my mom grew up together, and Magda and I had been friends since we were babies. It was like we had no choice but to be best friends. And the thing is, Magda's always been the one in charge. When we were little, she was the one who picked what games we were going to play and made up all the rules.

Magda has this way about her. Whether she's talking to a cute guy, or trying out the latest dance moves, she approaches everything *con mucho fuerte*. She's fearless. But going to Panama, living in a foreign country, learning how to speak Spanish *como una nativa* had given me a sense of confidence that I never had before. In some ways, I had become a little fearless myself.

I can tell that while Magda was glad to have me back,

she didn't know quite what to make of the new me. Sometimes, I saw her watching me, studying me, to see how I had changed. I knew that she was looking for something like those scenes in the movies where the quiet, plain librarian takes off her glasses and shakes her hair out of the bun on top of her head and becomes a beautiful siren. But the things that had changed about me were things that couldn't be seen.

Getting dressed for school in the morning, I gazed in the mirror and saw the same chocolate-brown skin, the same curly twists of hair, except now they were shoulder length. I was taller, but I was still skinny, with boobs like distant stars, invisible to the naked eye. I had changed, but the changing hadn't stopped. Tía China, my favorite aunt, said that fifteen was the year that I would become a young women and would no longer be a *jovencita*. That's why the *quince* is so important. In olden days, when a girl had her *quince*, she could get married! I couldn't imagine being married now or anytime soon. But I knew that a *quince* meant big things were on the way.

I had been waiting my whole life to be fifteen, to be a woman. I knew one birthday doesn't change your life, but a *quince* is different. On your fifteenth birthday, you're surrounded by your family and your friends and they've gathered to say, "You're grown and I see this in you. You're no longer a child and I won't treat you that way."

The bus pulled up and Magda and I took seats near the back. "Six months isn't that long," Magda said, referring to our spring birthdays. Magda was born the end of April. I was born the first of May. "My mom says it really takes a year to plan a proper *quince*."

"I like your eye shadow," I said, admiring the curve of shimmery lavender powder that covered her lids.

Magda smiled, her glossy purple lips turning upward. "Really? Thanks," she said, appreciatively. "You know I'm glad I didn't go out for drill team this year. I really need all my after-school time to plan for my *quince*."

"I wish there was an art club I could join," I said, opening my notebook to a watercolor that I had done for art appreciation class.

"What do you think?"

Magda took the notebook out of my hand and examined it for a good five minutes, making "hmmm" and "hrrmph" sounds throughout.

"Well, it looks a lot like a bowl of plums," she said. I grabbed the notebook back and laughed.

"Way to go, Sherlock," I said. "I was asking you whether or not it was a good picture."

She shrugged. "It's *fine*. You've always been good at

art. *Muevate*, this is our stop."

In the Junior Formal department, we tried on one dress after another. We could only take three dresses at a time into the dressing room, so we ran around like madwomen grabbing from the racks. Magda tried on a gorgeous midnight-blue dress with a fur collar.

"*Bonita, no?*" Magda asked, hopefully.

I nodded my head yes. "But it's too Russian princessy. You need a dress with more flavor."

Magda came out with a purple dress with a big bow in the back. She threw her hands up in the air like a movie star.

"No way," I said. "Too Goody Two-shoes."

"Why don't you try on some dresses?" Magda asked.

I rubbed my fingers together, the way our moms always do when they're talking about cash. "No dough-re-mi," I explained.

Magda just shrugged. "Whatever."

She tried on a blue dress with sequins, a pink dress with sequins, and a light green dress with sheer-illusion sleeves; it looked like the same kind of dress those champion ice-skater girls wear during the Winter Olympics. I wished there were an Olympic competiton for most exhaustive window shopping, 'cause Magda and I would win first place for sure.

For the umpteenth time, Magda tried on this long

black spandex-y dress with a strapless pearl bodice. It looked great on her. As the guys at our school say, her hips were bumpin'. But Magda's mom was so religious. Even if she let the clingy fabric slide, there was absolutely no way she was going to let Magda wear black for her *quince*. She could hardly stand the way Magda dressed already. *"Pero, niña,"* she always said when she saw Magda in head-to-toe black. "You know black is for funerals."

I wandered over to the other side of the store floor while Magda got dressed. There were so many beautiful dresses. My fingers instinctively reached for each price tag, then I quickly looked away and moved on. Then I saw a dress on a mannequin that I couldn't stop staring at. It was cranberry red, floor length, with spaghetti straps and a sheer-illusion waist.

"It's like an Oscar dress," Magda said, approvingly.

I jumped at the sound of her voice. "I didn't see you there," I said. *"Bellísima, no?"*

Magda jumped up on the box with the mannequin and threw both her arms in the air and posed. "I just want to thank all the little people. . . ." she said, in a fab British accent. Magda was great at accents. I just rolled my eyes.

"You'll have to step down," said a young saleswoman. She was about twenty-five, dressed in a black pantsuit and funky retro tortoiseshell eyeglasses.

"Would you like to try the dress on?" the saleswoman asked.

"Not me, my friend," Magda said, climbing down.

"What size?" the saleswoman asked me. I felt a little nervous then. I kept thinking that maybe I shouldn't be trying on dresses I had no money to buy.

"Size seven," I squeaked.

The saleswoman went to get the dress and I grabbed Magda by the sleeve.

"What am I *doing*?" I asked. "I can't afford this dress. I don't even know if I'm going to have a *quince*."

"It doesn't hurt to try it on," Magda said. *"No te preocupes."*

I took the dress from the saleswoman and entered the dressing room, pulling the velvet blue curtain closed. I undressed and stared for a second at my reflection in the mirror. I always thought the same thing about my skinny legs and puny breasts. Everything in the teen magazines was about how most girls want to be thin—some even starved themselves to do it. But in our neighborhood, guys seemed to like girls with round breasts and curves. "Can I get some fries to go with that shake?" they'd call out to my Tía China when we walked down the street. As much as it embarrassed me, there was a part of me that wanted them to call out the same things to me.

"Come on, *niña*," Magda called into the dressing room. "Today, not tomorrow."

I stepped from behind the curtain and self-consciously straightened the skirt of the dress.

"What do you think?" I asked.

"Amazing," Magda said. "You should buy it right now."

I felt my chest tighten and willed myself not to cry. Magda knew I didn't have the money to buy the dress. Sometimes it was like she said careless things on purpose.

"That dress is so beautiful on you," echoed the salesgirl, whose name tag said ANN. She straightened one of the straps while I admired myself in the mirror.

"You're so tall, you can pull off wearing so much red," Ann said. "Not to mention that it looks beautiful against your skin."

I agreed, pausing to turn and admire myself in the mirror. I held my hair back and imagined the *quince* crown on my head.

"It's perfect," Magda whispered.